"Clever and unique world bu[...] author who can write the heck [...]

—Lauren Dane, natio[...]

PRAISE FOR

Three Sinful Wishes

"*Three Sinful Wishes* made me laugh, made me cry, made me reach for the nearest fan—the perfect erotic romance!"

—Eve Berlin, author of *Desire's Edge*

"It is rare to find an author who draws you into sensual new worlds with characters who tug at your heartstrings. R. G. Alexander offers up paranormal romance at its finest!"

—Crystal Jordan, author of *Embrace the Night*

Possess Me

"Lush and sensual. Pure magic!" —Eden Bradley

"You will be fascinated by the spellbinding and magical imagination of author R. G. Alexander." —*The Romance Studio*

"Sultry days in the Big Easy get a lot steamier with three novellas wrapped around the legend of a voodoo spirit who can fulfill every darkest fantasy. All of these dovetailing stories are fun, hot, and romantic." —*RT Book Reviews*

"*Possess Me* is a hot and sexy read that took me to places I didn't know I wanted to go . . . R. G. Alexander is an author I love to read and *Possess Me* is no different. I am enraptured by her world and her characters and wouldn't mind seeing more of her New Orleans."
—*Joyfully Reviewed*

"This erotic novel was smoking hot—a perfect summer read set in my favorite city, New Orleans . . . I honestly couldn't put this book down. It was wonderful to read something so delightfully different and deliciously magical. Sensual, seductive, and filled with sexy—if you like paranormal erotica, this book's for you."
—*Fangtastic Books* (4.5 fangs)

"As this was my first time reading R. G. Alexander, I am happy to report I look forward to more of her work in the future!"
—*Night Owl Reviews*

"*Possess Me* is erotic with a capital O. And so sweet and vivid! Steamy sex and true emotion? So rare. So lovely. So addictive! . . . I haven't been this enamored of a book since I began Kresley Cole's Immortals After Dark series. You can be assured I'll be stocking up with R. G. Alexander's backlist and rereading *Possess Me* anytime I need a little heat to keep me warm at night."
—*Bitten by Books*

"*Possess Me* . . . takes you on a sultry trip, laced with mystical and otherworldly touches, through the heart of New Orleans. I've long been a fan of R. G. Alexander's work . . . [and she] brings her brilliant storytelling and her knack for the wickedly sexy to the table."
—*Romance Junkies*

Heat titles by R. G. Alexander

POSSESS ME

THREE SINFUL WISHES

TEMPT ME

TEMPT ME

R. G. ALEXANDER

HEAT | NEW YORK

THE BERKLEY PUBLISHING GROUP
Published by the Penguin Group
Penguin Group (USA) Inc.
375 Hudson Street, New York, New York 10014, USA
Penguin Group (Canada), 90 Eglinton Avenue East, Suite 700, Toronto, Ontario M4P 2Y3, Canada
(a division of Pearson Penguin Canada Inc.)
Penguin Books Ltd., 80 Strand, London WC2R 0RL, England
Penguin Group Ireland, 25 St. Stephen's Green, Dublin 2, Ireland (a division of Penguin Books Ltd.)
Penguin Group (Australia), 250 Camberwell Road, Camberwell, Victoria 3124, Australia
(a division of Pearson Australia Group Pty. Ltd.)
Penguin Books India Pvt. Ltd., 11 Community Centre, Panchsheel Park, New Delhi—110 017, India
Penguin Group (NZ), 67 Apollo Drive, Rosedale, Auckland 0632, New Zealand
(a division of Pearson New Zealand Ltd.)
Penguin Books (South Africa) (Pty.) Ltd., 24 Sturdee Avenue, Rosebank, Johannesburg 2196,
South Africa

Penguin Books Ltd., Registered Offices: 80 Strand, London WC2R 0RL, England

This book is an original publication of The Berkley Publishing Group.

Copyright © 2011 by R. G. Alexander.
Cover art by Tony Mauro.
Cover design by Rita Frangie.
Text design by Kristin del Rosario.

PRINTING HISTORY
Heat trade paperback edition / November 2011

Library of Congress Cataloging-in-Publication Data

Alexander, R. G., (date)-
    Tempt me / R. G. Alexander. — Heat trade paperback ed.
        p.   cm.
    ISBN 978-0-425-24333-6
    1. Twins—Fiction.   2. Reconciliation—Fiction.   3. Loa (Spirits)—Fiction.   4. Voodooism—Fiction.
5. New Orleans (La.)—Fiction.   I. Title.
    PS3601.L3545T46   2011
    813'.6—dc22
                            2011028160

PRINTED IN THE UNITED STATES OF AMERICA

10   9   8   7   6   5   4   3   2   1

ACKNOWLEDGMENTS

For Cookie: Love is the reason. To the best agent in the known universe, Roberta, and my amazing editor, Kate, who both believed in me and the world Bone Daddy made enough that they let me return to play in it. To my Smutketeers, my dearest friends, the glorious Eden Bradley and Robin L. Rotham, for their red pens and hand holding. To the talented Bryan W. for having mad RPG knowledge and giving me a name to fit Gabriel's ability. A huge and heartfelt dedication to the real Ive and Kelly . . . yes, you . . . for being fantastic and for campaigning so enthusiastically for a Bone Daddy Hunt that you became my inspiration.

Finally, again and always, to New Orleans, Louisiana—you are so much more than just a party girl throwing beads. The more I know you, the deeper in love I fall.

CHAPTER 1

❧

"Care for another, angel?"

Gabriel nodded at the bartender, ignoring the blatant invitation in her eyes.

Angel. His smile was rich with self-mockery. If he'd ever been one, he'd fallen long ago.

The sexy blonde turned to refill his glass with amber ale, and the sight of his own reflection in the beveled mirrors made him wince. It had been a while since he'd seen himself. Too long, apparently. The first description that sprang to mind when he did was *pathetic drunk*.

Was this who he really was, then? Gabriel Toussaint Giodarno—just another lost soul?

Whoever it was he was glaring at needed a shave. Rough

shadows framed a sharp jaw, accentuating cheeks that had hollowed out in the last year. A diet of beer, scotch, and shame would do that to a man.

His dark hair curled around his ears and along the nape of his neck—the first time he'd let it grow out since he was sent to Catholic school at the tender age of nine. His heavy-lidded green eyes were bleary with exhaustion, and—his gaze narrowed—the skin above his left cheek was still tinged with yellow and blue from his encounter with that angry biker last week in a Tupelo bar.

Nearly all traces of his old reflection were gone. *He* was gone.

"You look like hell, Gabe. As usual."

Shit. He knew he was drunk, but he hadn't realized he'd had enough to start hallucinating again. He pushed his beer away and tapped on the glossy wooden counter. "Any coffee in this place?" Or, even better, some holy water?

The man beside him sighed. "I was hoping you'd head to Mambo Toussaint's or Michelle's instead of the nearest tavern. Why you keep gravitating to these shadow-filled places, I'll never know."

"Look, guy, I told you—those shadows aren't real," Gabriel muttered, keeping his eyes straight ahead and his voice down so the bartender wouldn't think he'd gone off the deep end. "*You* aren't real. Not a man. Not a ghost. Remember? *I* don't do that particular parlor trick. All the woo-woo genes went to my sister. You're just a figment of my imagination."

He lowered his head tiredly and shoved his hands through

his hair. "Shit, why couldn't my broken brain concoct a hot, breathy blonde to follow me around instead of a chatty, grungy man-child like you?" He sent said man-child a sideways glance. "I did what you wanted. I'm in New Orleans. Nothing has changed. Now, run along, shut the hell up, and leave me in peace."

He looked up and noticed the bartender was watching him and no longer smiling suggestively. She slid a cup of coffee in his direction, the suspicious look in her eyes clearly retracting any invitation they might have issued earlier. Then she hurried toward the other end of the bar and the safety of her regular customers.

Gabriel smirked. He'd run, too, if he could. Hell, he'd tried. But he couldn't escape the guilt that had kept him up nights, the inner demons stalking him. He'd even started seeing shadows where there should be none. Watching those shadows notice him. Follow him. Press on his heavy heart and twist his thoughts until there were only three avenues of escape: fighting, fucking, or getting blackout-drunk. Sometimes it took all three for him to feel human again. To regain control.

Four months ago the game had changed, and his mind brought out the big guns. His new buddy here. His walking, talking, invisible conscience. There could be no doubt now that he had truly gone around the bend.

Gabriel grimaced at the first rich taste of chicory, and glanced at his imaginary friend. He had no idea where he'd dreamed this guy up. A man in his twenties, with black hair that fell to his shoulders and blue eyes that were startling, framed by dark brows and a swarthy complexion. He wore a long dark trench coat, dirty khaki pants, and torn-up boots, looking like one of those disaffected adolescents Gabriel had silently scorned. Back when he'd been a globe-trotting, self-important businessman.

Had it been only a year ago that employees of his father's investment firm had cowered in fear before him? That Gabriel had taken pride in being known as the Dark Messenger, the smiling bearer of bad news and pink slips? What an evil jackass he'd been.

Maybe he was finally getting what he deserved.

"I can practically feel that self-pity you're wrapping yourself up in, Gabe. You're more stubborn than your sister, and that's saying something. Honestly, I have no idea why I got stuck with you."

He'd gotten stuck? Ha. "I apologize for inconveniencing you. Even my hallucinations can't stand me. There's a certain poetry to that, don't you think?"

"I'm not a hallucination, idiot. I'm real, with a name and everything. But you haven't asked my name, have you? You haven't asked about me, about the shadows—nothing. You need to stop fucking around, Gabe." The young man pounded on the bar in frustration. "I never swore before I met you, though I don't think the Virgin Mother herself would blame me. You came back here for a reason. You need to find out what you are. You need to see your family. Tell your mother what's been happening to you."

Not *who* he was. *What* he was. Gabriel already knew what

he wasn't. He was no angel. No *bon ange*, like his twin sister, who could see spirits. The one who had risked her soul for him, despite what he'd done to her. He was no loving son or loyal friend. And even though it felt like it right now, he was no ghost.

He wasn't sure about anything anymore, not even why he'd come back to New Orleans again. Other than to shut his invisible stalker up. The one no one else saw. The one who could so conveniently appear and disappear at will.

If only Gabriel could disappear that easily, along with the memory of what he'd done—what he'd almost done—to Mimi. Michelle. His sister.

Djab. That was the name his mother had called the thing that had taken over his body last year. A dark entity, sometimes controlled by voodoo sorcerers she named *bokors*. *Djab* were wild spirits that, when left to their own devices, could wreak havoc on weaker humans.

Weak. That wasn't a word Gabriel had ever associated with himself until it happened. How easily it had taken him over. He'd been angry at the awkward reunion with his mother, and when Michelle had shown up, injured and so distant, he'd blamed her. In his anger, he'd wished *she'd* been the one the priests had beaten, the one who'd been ripped from their mother and told everything she knew, everything she loved, was no longer hers. His need for vengeance had made him the perfect target.

Gabriel took a deep drink, the hot coffee scalding his tongue, his knuckles white around the porcelain mug. As if it were yesterday, he could recall the feeling of being trapped in his own mind, of screaming and shouting in disbelief as something else took over his body.

His hands tying up his sister. *His* mouth speaking words so offensive to his soul that he wished he could claw them out with his bare hands.

How could she ever forgive him for that? How could he forgive himself? He shook his head, coming back to the conversation. "I know what I am. And they are all better off without me. You can add *delusional* to the list of reasons why."

"That does it."

Gabriel nearly slid off his stool when the bartender appeared across from him once more and purred appreciatively, "Didn't see *you* come in, lover. What can I get for you?"

He blinked. Déjà vu. "What? Are you talking to me?"

She rolled her eyes. "Of course not, silly; you've been here for hours. And I'm really glad you decided to have that coffee, by the way." Then she looked over Gabriel's shoulder and batted her eyelashes. "I'm talking to your cute young friend."

He followed her gaze, then turned back to the bartender. "Who do you see behind me?" When she hesitated, Gabriel leaned closer. "It's important. Describe him."

She tilted her head, her blonde ponytail swinging softly behind her. "O-kay, I'll play. I see a sexy slice of cheesecake with dark hair and stunning blue eyes." Her own eyes widened. "And he blushes? Oh, baby, what's your name, what's your sign, and where have you been all my life?"

Black spots and stars blurred Gabriel's view as he glanced back at the blushing figment behind him. The figment someone else had just described. She *saw* him?

He heard the bartender's worried voice as if she were speaking through static. "Oh, damn. Listen, lover, if your friend is about to throw up or something, get him outta here. I'm the only one on tonight and I refuse to clean that up."

Gabriel felt hands hoist him up as if he were weightless and drag him toward the back door that led to a narrow alley.

He pushed away and fell to his knees, retching. He leaned his head against the rough wall, a rasping laugh escaping his raw throat. "So this is what rock bottom looks like. I always wondered."

"Congratulations, Gabe. As usual, you set a goal and you reached it. Your father would be so proud."

Gabriel pulled himself up once more and turned, rage suddenly welling up inside him. "You don't know shit about my father. But I just set another goal. If other people can see you, that means you're real. And if you're real, I can kick your ass."

The tall man's lips quirked. "You can try. The shape you're in? I think I can take you." He crossed his arms and shook his head. "You used to be a believer, Gabe. Even when you couldn't see me, when Mimi was the only one who could, you believed I was there. I never thought you'd turn out like this."

He believed . . . even when *Mimi* could see him? "Who the fuck *are* you?"

His illusion's hands rose up to the sky, as if in prayer. "Hallelujah. I think he's finally waking up." Unearthly blue eyes pierced him with their solemn expression. "The name is Emmanuel."

Gabriel scoffed, but he felt the name like a kick in the chest, making it hard to breathe. "Emmanuel was a child. A *ghost* child. I told you my sister has that gift, not me. But even I know ghosts don't age."

Emmanuel nodded. "You're right. That isn't your gift." He shrugged. "But all the same, I *am* Emmanuel. How else would I know you cracked your tooth when you fell chasing after Ben and your sister in the back of my old house? The same day you told your father you were playing with spirits for the first time."

Gabriel remembered. How could he forget? That was the day everything had started going to shit.

"If you're Emmanuel, and I can't see ghosts, then how can I see you?"

The younger man was suddenly right beside him, so close he could feel his breath. His expression was tinged with pain and regret. They were emotions Gabriel knew well. "You can see me, Gabriel, because I am not a ghost. I'm no longer anything I was. And neither are you. But I've faced more than a few of *my* monsters. It's time for you to face yours. You need to understand what's happening to you, before you lose yourself completely to the darkness."

This was some sort of twisted joke. Gabriel closed his eyes and saw a flash of a memory. Father Leon, the priest who had taken special delight in punishing him, tormenting him with images of his sister and mother burning in Lucifer's inferno for eternity. Warning him that he would join them if he didn't purge himself of his family's evil. Warning him that he would be taken by the darkness.

Even then, there was a small part of the young Gabriel who would have taken that punishment, would have burned, if only he could be with his family again. His mother. If only he could have been like his twin, Mimi. Special.

He felt like he was going to be sick again. This couldn't be happening. He needed to get out of this cursed city. "Fuck the coffee. I need another drink, maybe two, and then I'll be on the next flight out of town. As far away as I can get."

Gabriel took a step toward the bar's back door, but Emmanuel was there before he could reach for the knob.

He shook his head. "Stubborn ass. This is for your own good."

Gabriel saw Emmanuel pull back his fist and swore when it connected with his flesh. For a ghost, he had a powerful right hook.

He was falling to the ground again, hearing Emmanuel before he hit the cobblestone pavement.

"You'll thank me for this, Gabe. Eventually."

Gratitude wasn't on his mind as the hard ground jarred his bones. His ears rang with the power of the physical blow he'd just received from his imaginary pest. No, it wasn't gratitude causing the red haze of anger and pain to blind his vision.

It was the need for revenge.

As soon as he could get up again, Emmanuel would learn what everyone who'd ever gotten on the wrong side of Gabriel knew. Clichéd but true . . .

Payback was a bitch.

* * *

THEY WERE TALKING ABOUT *HIM*.

Angelique Rousseau grabbed a candied pecan but paused before slipping it into her mouth. She'd been planning on announcing her presence, but she didn't want to miss the hushed discussion between her sister-in-law Allegra and Michelle Toussaint. Not when they were whispering about her current obsession, Michelle's elusive brother, Gabriel.

Michelle's sigh drifted into the kitchen from the formal dining room as Angelique hopped quietly onto the marble island. "Mama said she heard a knock on her door at three in the morning. Apparently he was bloodied up and falling-down drunk, with no idea how he'd gotten to her house."

"He's been here a week and he hasn't told anyone why he came back? Has he said *anything*?" Allegra sounded worried and more than a little tired. Angelique wondered if her unborn niece or nephew might have something to do with that.

The little troublemaker. Not even born and it was already driving its mother up the hormonal wall, not to mention putting a cramp in Auntie Angelique's social life.

She hadn't had *any* time to herself from the moment she got home. Instead she'd been mobbed at every turn by Toussaints and Adairs. Tasked with taking her mother to one gathering after another, all so Theresa Rousseau could get to know her new extended family better before the baby came.

It was a strange clan they'd created. The three families had known one another forever, but at a comfortable distance. Lately, however, there'd been a contagious bout of the dangerous disease called matrimony. First her brother and Allegra, then Michelle and Ben Adair and their friends Bethany and BD. It was enough to make Angelique twitchy. As if she didn't have enough trouble dealing with her immediate family's nosy ways. At least they weren't as focused on her . . . for the moment. They were all too busy closing ranks around Michelle since her twin brother, Gabriel, had come home.

Angelique was dying to find out why.

Michelle spoke again, answering Allegra's question. "He's barely said a word. Though a few days ago he did ask me some unusual questions. It was . . . an odd conversation, and I'm not sure he was actually listening. He just kept glaring over my shoulder. Other than that, every time I've stopped by the house, he's been in his bedroom. Honestly, I'll be surprised if he comes tonight, but Mama did say he promised."

Was that why Angelique had decided to show up for dinner tonight—because Gabriel Toussaint had promised to be here? Why she'd changed her mind and accepted Allegra's transparently halfhearted invitation, even though her mother wasn't invited? Even though she'd had a chance for one night's reprieve, free of family, free to enjoy herself and get away from all this loving togetherness?

She knew the answer was yes. Gabriel's presence had changed everything. Since she'd seen him a few days ago, when she and her mother had stopped by the Toussaint family home, he was all she could think about.

He'd stalked into the room, seemingly unaware that he

wasn't alone. His shirt had been unbuttoned to reveal a line of golden skin and muscle that set her mouth watering. His hair was mussed, his jaw set, and to Angelique he'd looked like one hot, delicious mess. Ruffled, brooding, and sexy. Everything about him screamed bad boy. It was a quality the rebellious part of her couldn't help but find attractive.

But it was more than that. The moment he turned his head and snared her gaze, she experienced a raw wave of need unlike any she'd ever known, heat washing over her body and nearly buckling her knees.

She'd held her breath as he studied her. Her fertile imagination took over, making her breathless as she wondered if he felt the same intense desire that she did.

But then he seemed to notice the other women in the room. She'd hoped he would look her way again, but he'd just scowled, nodded tersely to acknowledge his mother, then turned and walked out without a word.

Mambo Toussaint had made hurried apologies, but Angelique barely heard them. It took every ounce of her restraint not to follow him back down the hallway. To take him to task for his manners . . . or rub herself against him like a cat; she wasn't sure which.

She'd gone home that night, irrationally angry with the rude man who'd turned on some switch in her body that couldn't be shut off. She'd touched herself, rubbing her clit and slipping her fingers deep inside her sex, fantasizing about him, coming again and again without true relief.

Feeling the need well up inside her even now, she squirmed

on the countertop. Just thinking about seeing him tonight was making her crazy.

That *was* why she'd come. It was too tempting to resist. She hadn't been able to stop fantasizing about him and she wanted to know more. To find out why everyone was so worried about his homecoming.

Hell, she wasn't sure she'd care if she knew. She just wanted to see him again.

"You are now officially my favorite Rousseau, *cher*. Your brother would never dream of being this sneaky. Trust me, I know him well. However, you lose some points by eating all my pecans."

Angelique nearly fell off her perch at the rich male voice behind her. "BD, I didn't see you there."

Speaking of impossibly gorgeous bad boys. She silently corrected herself. Reformed bad boy. Reformed, reborn, and happily married.

Angelique blushed while she studied him. Each time she saw him, it struck her that he was like living art. If she weren't so oddly enamored with Gabriel, he would definitely be her favorite fantasy.

He'd literally walked out of history, and he was nearly too beautiful to be real. Amber eyes with long, dark lashes. Skin like honey and full lips that always looked freshly kissed.

Too pretty, his wife, Bethany, always teased him. And it was true. But Angelique wasn't just fascinated with his looks. It was what he was, or what he'd been, that entranced her.

Bone Daddy. A sexual Loa. A voodoo spirit. Sort of. He'd

been around a few hundred years, showing up for voodoo practitioners who needed aid in love and lust spells, making those he "rode" irresistible. Until he'd fallen in love himself and gotten a second chance.

He was also the reason her brother had changed so much after their father's death eight years ago. Why Celestin had gone from her playful, charming older brother to a distant, melancholy womanizer. It had been because of Bone Daddy and the deal her brother had made with the spirit to protect his family. To protect her.

Now, though she still wasn't sure how, the Loa was human. And before she could work up a good mad on her brother's behalf, Celestin had made it clear to his mother and sisters that BD was a friend. More than that. One of the family. That decree, combined with BD's undeniable warmth and charm, made it impossible to do anything other than love him.

An ex-Loa in her growing family. It was the most exciting thing that had happened in her life so far. Well, maybe the second-most exciting thing.

"You didn't see me? I wonder why." BD smiled delightedly, dazzling her into silence. "Could it be you were too focused on the gossip du jour? The return of the eternally grumpy twin?"

Angelique felt her lips tilt even as her blush deepened. "My family has a lot of secrets. Maybe this is the only way I can find anything out. Or maybe I was just trying to swipe all the good snacks."

"Bah. I know your type. Hell, I *am* your type, *cher*. A trouble magnet." He shook his head, understanding bright in his beautiful eyes. "And I can see you are looking for trouble tonight. Don't deny it. Your brother would be sad to think he wasn't the reason you decided to join us this evening. Although I'm not sure Gabriel is ready for a wildcat like you."

How did he know? How could he possibly know? "I'm not sure what you're talking about, but whatever it is, I'm innocent."

BD made a face when Angelique batted her eyelashes. "I applaud your acting, *cher*, as well as your stealth, but it's wasted on me. Desire was my job long before you were born. I've seen what lengths men and women go to taste that forbidden fruit. Now, before you get us both in trouble, you should get down. Your brother is on his way inside as we speak."

The thought of her big brother catching her in the act of eavesdropping had her hopping off the kitchen island swiftly, and she gave BD a quick, impulsive hug. "Thanks for the heads-up."

He chuckled, squeezing her shoulders gently before pulling back to look down at her. "Anytime, *cher*." His golden gaze fell to her neck and his expression changed suddenly. "Do me a favor in return, yes? Don't take that necklace off."

Angelique's brow furrowed as she reached up to fiddle with the thin, golden cross her mother had given her at her baptism. "Why?"

BD opened his mouth to respond, but the sound of heavy footsteps behind him stopped him from answering.

"Little one, I'm glad you came." Celestin Rousseau beamed

at her happily, his arms filled with food from Allegra's favorite corner restaurant. "I brought dinner. A little bit of everything, so I hope you're hungry."

His relaxed, easygoing expression was so different from the brother she'd known most of her adult life that it still jarred her. She knew it was his wife and unborn child, as well as his freedom from the curse their father had forced on him, that had changed him. She couldn't be happier for him, but it was a big adjustment.

"I'm starving. And of course I came. An evening without Mom trying to get me to move into the new house her loving son bought for her? Asking me when I was going to give her grandchildren like her daughter-in-law? I couldn't pass that up."

Her brother snorted, setting several bags down on the counter where she'd been sitting moments before. "Can you blame her? Her nest is empty. All her children growing up and flying away. Patricia moved to North Carolina with her husband this year; you came home from school and decided to stay in that old, musty apartment we grew up in rather than the new room she decorated with you in mind . . ." He trailed off, making a face as BD guffawed.

"Not even a father yet and you already do guilt so well, *mon ami*."

Angelique nodded emphatically. "He's a natural, all right. I'm a grown woman with a college degree and a normal sex drive. I love you both, but I do *not* want to move back in with my mommy."

Celestin held up his hands in surrender. "And the last thing

I want to hear about is my baby sister's sex drive, adult or not. You win. I won't mention it again."

"Thank you."

BD's laughter stopped the conversation in the other room and Angelique sighed. She'd wanted to find out more about Gabriel before he came.

Allegra raised her voice from the other room. "BD? Is my husband with you? I'd get up but his child has turned me into a giant, immovable water buffalo with cankles."

Celestin's smile grew even more incandescent. "Duty calls. Coming, *bebe*." He ruffled Angelique's curls and handed her the last small bag he carried in his hand. "Could you put her ice cream in the freezer before it melts, and start setting the table, little one?" Then he was gone.

BD was chuckling again. "That boy is going to be a great daddy."

Angelique rolled her eyes, closing the freezer and opening drawers in search of utensils. "If *great* is another word for bossy, overprotective, and way up in the poor child's Kool-Aid, then sure. Tell me, do ex–sex spirits know where they keep the silverware around here?"

He came up beside her and pointed to a drawer while he opened the cabinet over her head where the plates were kept. "I know a lot of things. My wife is determined I become a truly modern man. I can even do laundry now."

He winked at her and she laughed, charmed. Too bad he was taken. There was just something about him . . .

"Am I late?"

The voice sent the pile of forks in her hand clattering to the counter. Her heart started to pound, her body reacting the way it did every time he came to mind. All thoughts of the captivating BD disappeared.

Gabriel had arrived.

CHAPTER 2

"Look who i found hanging around outside." A woman with long dark hair skirted her way around Michelle's brother as she spoke, allowing herself to be swept up in BD's embrace.

"Blue Eyes, I've missed you. Is everything okay?"

Bethany sent her husband a strange expression, nodding quickly before stepping away from him. "Fine. Everything's fine. And something smells delicious."

Angelique noticed Bethany's evasion, but she was too focused on the man who joined her to pay it much attention.

He was here. He'd come.

BD nodded in Gabriel's direction over Bethany's head. "Your sister will be glad you're here."

"We'll see. More to the point, the Mambo will. I've recently learned that denying my mother's requests is a dangerous endeavor. In more ways than one."

His voice. The sexy rasp of it, the slight accent, made Angelique bite her lip. She'd heard him on the phone yesterday, when she'd called under the guise of asking Mambo Toussaint a question for her mother. He'd been terse and monosyllabic, but by the time he'd hung up Angelique's body had reacted as though he'd touched her. Caressed her.

BD huffed out a sound of agreement. "You don't have to tell me. Annemarie Toussaint is a powerful priestess. The Loa watch over her . . . and everyone she loves."

The two men stared at each other in tense silence. Why did BD's words sound like both a warning and a peace offering? And why, Angelique sighed, did she still feel as if she were missing a crucial bit of information that everyone else knew about but her?

Michelle entered the kitchen, Ben following close behind her. "Gabriel, you're here."

He wasn't smiling as his sister embraced him, though it was obvious he tried. Angelique noticed his awkwardness as his hands lifted to pat his sister's back. This was not a man used to affection.

What a sad thought.

Ben saved him, pulling Michelle back against him and reaching out to shake Gabriel's hand. "Hey, brother, been hearing the rumor you were back in town. Glad to see it's true. And I'm happy you decided to accept our invitation."

Gabriel nodded, and Angelique held her breath as his gaze met hers. Just like before, the other people in the room disappeared until all she could see, all she knew, was him. Why did he affect her like this?

His sparkling green eyes narrowed, unblinking for a long, breathless moment. Two. Then he looked away, responding to Ben without acknowledging her presence.

"Yes, well, I won't be here for long."

Ben frowned, releasing Gabriel's hand slowly, his expression thoughtful. Suspicious.

An uneasy silence settled over the kitchen, and Gabriel shifted, as if uncomfortable with all the attention.

She hoped he was uncomfortable, the jerk. Did he learn rude from his father's side of the family? This was the third time he'd dismissed her in as many days. She'd spent the week fantasizing about the man, and he'd never even said hello.

It was hard on a girl's ego to go so instantly gaga over someone who wouldn't give you the time of day. Yet something about his almost defiant avoidance of her made her doubt its veracity.

It wasn't just her he was steering clear of; that much was apparent to her now. He seemed intent on keeping everyone off-kilter. On pushing them all away. She wondered why he had bothered coming back when he clearly didn't want to be here. Wondered what it would take to get him to react to her.

Angelique was no masochist. It wasn't her style to chase after hopeless cases. She had a healthy dose of self-confidence to go along with her Rousseau pride. She knew men liked what they saw when they looked at her, what they noticed. That though they had often commented on her long, russet-brown curls, her dimples, and her "kissable" mouth, that wasn't—in their eyes— her appeal.

It was her breasts.

They *were* good breasts. Perky and proud, defying gravity despite their fullness. A fullness accentuated by her small waist and the sway of her curving hips. She wasn't a slender, airbrushed beauty. She was real. All debate to the contrary, she'd never met a man who wouldn't rather have a handful of natural than silicone and bone.

She pulled her shoulders back and caught his attention shift, the muscle at his temple twitching. She had to hold in a small whoop of triumph. Despite how he was trying to ignore her, he couldn't. Not completely. It was a start.

"Now that the guest of honor has arrived, can we eat? The pregnant woman is hungry." Allegra's voice coming from the door to the dining room broke the tension, and everyone laughed and moved in her direction.

Only one person still looked as coiled up as a cornered rattlesnake, giving off the unmistakable air of leave-me-the-hell-alone. But Angelique knew she wasn't going to be able to.

It wasn't in her nature.

"You sure you're okay, *cher*?"

Angelique hid her smile behind her water glass as she noticed the beautiful BD continuing to worry over his bride throughout the meal. Bethany had come to New Orleans to help Michelle and Ben do some research on the last occupants of the mansion . . . and had won the heart of Bone Daddy. The "Love Doctor of the Big Easy" was well and truly caught, and he didn't look like he had any interest in getting away.

Bethany smiled, but even to Angelique, who was only now getting to know her, it looked off. "We aren't here to talk about me. Not right now. We're here to welcome Gabriel home, and to celebrate Allegra and Rousseau's upcoming home birth. Michelle and I are going to be the best midwives you've ever seen. I must have read thirty books on the subject so far."

"Thank you, Bethany." Allegra's eyes grew misty. "I know you're going to do a great job."

"Midwives? You're having the baby at your house?"

Angelique nibbled on a piece of corn bread as she watched Allegra lean forward with an excited smile to answer Gabriel's question. "Actually, we're doing it right here, at Ben and Michelle's. I can't wait."

Gabriel paled and glanced down at his plate. "Here?"

Angelique choked on her corn bread and he glared in her direction. "She didn't mean in the dining room." She lifted an eyebrow, unfazed. "Although it's not a *bad* idea. This table is certainly big enough."

Allegra snorted. "I wasn't planning on giving birth between courses, Gabriel. Don't let our new college graduate scare you."

Celestin leaned over and tugged on one of Angelique's curls. "I love hearing that. College graduate. The first in our family. And you made the top of your class, right?"

She batted his hand away and glanced at Gabriel through

her lashes. Since the meal started she'd been planning his seduction. The last thing she wanted was for him to see her as a child. Now her brother was one step away from showing baby pictures. *That* would make her evening perfect.

Ben took pity on her. "What was it you got your degree in? I keep thinking it's sassin' back, but I don't know if they offer that major at LSU yet."

Angelique stuck out her tongue. "Very funny. You know it was environmental engineering. Besides"—she pointed at him with her fork—"I don't need a class on sass. I was taught by the master."

Gabriel looked up at that, directly at Angelique, with an expression that was insultingly reminiscent of disbelief. "Interesting."

Angelique knew what he wasn't saying. She'd heard it before. Most of the guys she'd dated had said something to the effect of, "An engineer? I wouldn't have guessed. Teacher, baker, or salsa dancer, maybe. Not engineer." Why would he be any different?

She narrowed her gaze warningly. "Katrina hit during my first semester. When the levees failed, I wondered why. The more I learned about the erosion and the design flaws, the more I wanted to know. When I found out about the work that was needed in wetland preservation and coastline restoration, well . . ." She shared a smile with Celestin. "Being our mother's child, I wanted to fix it."

Bethany looked around her husband, an expression of true

interest relaxing her features. "Allegra told me you also minored in Southern folklore. A girl after my own multitasking heart."

Angelique nodded. "At first I thought it would be an easy A. Growing up here, I knew it all, right? But there's more tall tales and folk legends in and around Louisiana than I imagined. It was fascinating." She laughed. "Although we spent a lot of time focusing on my professor's personal passion. He knew as much about the Loup Garou, or Rougarou as he called them, as I expect Mambo Toussaint knows about voodoo."

Ben shushed her and glanced around the room with a humorous impression of paranoia. "Rousseau, you'd better tell your little sister that there is no one, *anywhere*, who knows about anything as well as my mama-in-law knows about voodoo. She may be listening."

BD chuckled. "Wouldn't put it past her, or your mama, Adair. Those two are dangerous." He winked at Angelique. "I should say those three now. The Mamas have officially added another member to their elite club, haven't they? By all accounts your mother is more than holding her own."

Grinning, Angelique popped a barbecued shrimp between her lips. Her mother, Theresa, had always shied away from her husband's voodoo religion as well as her own family's history with Santeria. She'd never spoken of it, had simply gone to church each week, volunteered, and made sure to have her babies crosses blessed by at least one Catholic priest. It had been her way to protect her children from their father's darker practices. That was why Angelique and her siblings were so surprised and, yes, relieved that she was getting along with the empath Elise Adair and the voodoo priestess Mambo Toussaint. In fact, she'd been spending so much time with them that Celestin had wondered aloud the other day if the Mamas were up to no good.

She swallowed. "My mistake, Ben. But my professor, while nowhere near as knowledgeable as Michelle's mama, *was* a font of information on the subject of werewolves."

Celestin looked down at his sister, grimacing. "Werewolves, huh? I never understood that particular story. I always had a hard time believing there were Loup Garou mushing around in the bayou. A killer gator, maybe, but a dog-boy?" He shook his head.

Gabriel's scratchy voice had a condescending tone. "I think we have enough to believe in as it is in this group without adding fairy tales about wolf-men to the list. What are they teaching kids in school these days? Next you'll be telling me there are vampires and unicorns."

Angelique lifted her chin at his obvious dismissal. Kids, huh? She had a sudden, mad desire to fling one of the plantains on her plate at his forehead. But as satisfying as that would be, it would serve only to prove him right. The jerk. "I'm sure education has changed dramatically in the last few decades, since you . . . *matriculated*? Is that the word they used back then? And you're probably right. Just because a sexy professor spun stories about werewolves, Loa, and spirit possessions doesn't mean any of that is true, right? I mean, everyone here knows none of *that* exists."

Gabriel stared at her in stony silence, then scraped back his chair. "Excuse me. I need some air."

He strode away from the table like the devil was on his heels. Maybe she was a masochist, after all, because all she wanted to do was follow him.

She bit her lip when she saw Ben and Michelle share a speaking look. "Was it something I said?"

"It's okay, little one. No one told you." Celestin spoke in a low voice beside her. "Michelle's brother is . . . Well, he's been through a lot."

A frustrated Michelle slapped the table with the palm of her hand. "I don't care what he's been through. He's being an ass, and I think I should go talk to him." Her brows drew together in obvious concern. "Maybe he'll tell me what's wrong this time."

Ben covered her hand with his own. "Mimi, you know what's wrong. After what happened last year . . . that he came home to face it at all, to face you, shows he's trying."

"What happened last year?"

Every gaze turned to Angelique at her question. They all wore the same hesitant expressions. Secretive.

What on earth had Gabriel done to have everyone speaking in riddles and whispers?

Whatever *had* happened, it must have been important. She wondered if it had anything to do with Michelle's and Ben's abilities.

Since she'd been home, Angelique had spent a lot of time with Allegra and Michelle, and along with feeling an instant camaraderie with the sassy Toussaint, she'd learned about Michelle's ability to see ghosts.

She'd already known Ben's talent. That he could see into anyone's mind with a touch. She'd always thought it was a magic trick, one he'd shown her several times when she was a child. Maybe that was why she was taking all this so well. This new magical reality. In one way or another, whether she'd known it or not, it had always been a part of her life.

Allegra pushed back her chair, shooing away Celestin when he tried to help her to her feet. "Let's give him a little more time. All of us together at once can be overwhelming in the best of circumstances. Now, who wants to help me clear the table?"

"*Bebe*, don't you dare. That's why I'm here." Celestin took the plate from her hand and gestured to Ben, who stood as well.

"I wouldn't want to face the Mamas if they found out I let my pregnant guest clean up in my house." Ben winked at her, filling his hands with the take-out boxes and plates in front of him.

Allegra made a face. "I'm not a guest and you know it. And being pregnant doesn't mean I can't wash the dishes."

Michelle, who had gotten up along with everyone else, placed her palm over Allegra's forehead. "You must be feverish, child. You have men waiting on you hand and foot and you want to *argue* about it? If I were pregnant, I'd be putting you to shame."

Ben stilled, sending his wife a sizzling look. "I'd be willing to beg to see that, Mimi."

"Well, I'm a guest, too. And I'm perfectly fine letting the men do all the work," Angelique muttered, reminding them they still had company.

Ben shook his finger at her playfully. "Sassy and spoiled. Just as I suspected."

The rest of them headed out of the dining room in a whirlwind of chatter and clinking china, leaving her behind with BD and Bethany. They were speaking so intently to each other that they'd barely noticed anyone had gone.

"Blue Eyes, tell me what's wrong. You know you can't lie to me."

Bethany shook her head. "Nothing is wrong. It's just, well . . ."

She sent a pleading glance in Angelique's direction. Even for a natural eavesdropper, it was an easy look to interpret. She pushed back her chair and got to her feet. "Speaking of air, I think I'll get a little myself and leave you two alone."

BD raised a speculative brow but Bethany just smiled in absentminded thanks.

She should really be thanking *them*. They'd given her exactly the excuse she needed to disappear, a fact BD no doubt suspected. She headed down the hall, away from the kitchen, before anyone else could notice.

The way Gabriel had gone.

He'd been headed outside. To the sprawling backyard thick with oak and magnolia trees . . . and happy memories.

She opened the glass-paneled doors that led outside, smelled the sweet, damp grass and magnolia blossoms, but saw no sign of her elusive prey. She took the path to the pristinely white gazebo, reaching out to skim her fingers along the wood grain when she reached it.

This was where Celestin and Allegra had gotten married. Angelique remembered how beautiful everything was. She'd cried to see her brother so happy, and, she was honest enough to admit to herself, she'd been more than a little envious. Not because of the beautiful ceremony, but the utter contentment and joy that shone like a halo around the couple. They knew what they wanted, where they were going, and that they would get there together.

She would give anything to be that sure. Someday. Right now she was just interested in how Gabriel made her feel. She had no illusions about those feelings. They weren't sweet and romantic. They were agitated and restless. Shameless.

She was shameless. She should probably go back inside before he realized she'd followed him out here like a hopeless puppy. Maybe go out and look for a handsome, low-maintenance tourist on Bourbon Street to let off some of this steam. Though she had a feeling it wouldn't do any good. Her inner desires were very specific. They wanted Gabriel.

"Why don't you just leave me the fuck alone?"

Angelique stumbled backward at the insult that seemed to be a response to her thoughts, and saw Gabriel standing beside the tree out of sight of the house.

That did it.

"Excuse me?"

Gabriel swore and spun around. Noticing her standing by the gazebo, he swore again. "I didn't see you there. I didn't mean— I was talking to . . . myself." He sighed and ran a hand through his already tousled hair. "I'm truly sorry if I offended you. It's a bad habit of mine."

She took a step closer, arms crossed defensively at her waist. "You seem to have a lot of those."

"Huh?"

"Bad habits," she clarified. "Drinking. Fighting. Offending people. And you talk to yourself, too."

He tilted his head, green eyes gleaming at her through the darkness. "Been listening to gossip, little girl? I don't think you pressed your ear to the keyhole long enough. Otherwise you wouldn't be out here. Go back inside, where it's safe."

She ignored the warning in his tone and sighed. "Angelique. In case you were wondering, since you never bothered with introductions, that's my name." She walked over to the tree and leaned against it, feeling the bark scrape against her back. "And I'm no little girl, as you can plainly see. I'm also not stupid." She made a face. "Top of my class. So who was it you were you talking to?"

Gabriel looked distracted. "What?"

She shrugged. "I'm not assuming. Trust me. Personally I'd love it if there were someone besides me who hadn't been intimately involved with something supernatural. Then I wouldn't feel so left out. But your mother is a mambo, your sister can see ghosts, and you two *are* twins . . ." She let the sentence dangle, biting her lip when he flinched.

She could see the barriers come up across his handsome face. She'd hit a nerve.

"Doing a paper for that sexy professor on the unusual Toussaint lineage? Following up the Loup Garou with ghosts and possession? Wouldn't you rather look at your own family line? You should ask your brother what life was like being ridden by a fuck-hungry spirit because your father liked to dabble in the darkness and had an eye for the ladies." Gabriel's smile was sharp, adding to the sting. "The eavesdropping is so much more interesting at my mother's house. You should try it."

DAMN, HE WAS A BASTARD. HE'D BARELY COME HOME AND already his sister was defensive, his mother disappointed, and now he was purposely trying to hurt this innocent.

This young, succulent, luscious little innocent in snug blue jeans and an off-the-shoulder peasant blouse. She made him feel like an old pervert. Like a kid with his first hard-on. He couldn't tear his gaze from the sweep of those smooth, bared shoulders. Couldn't keep himself from noticing the way the fabric fell against the firm rise of those unconfined, lush breasts.

Shit. If Little Miss Hot Coed was so clever, she should be smart enough to stay far away from him.

"Keep going," Emmanuel taunted, reminding Gabriel of his presence. "Your obvious charm is sure to win her over. The cleavage leering is really working, too. I know *my* heart's all atwitter."

Gabriel gritted his teeth, trying not to look at the tall man lounging, unseen, beside Angelique. Emmanuel had barely left him alone since he'd woken up with a hangover and a swollen jaw in his mother's house.

He wouldn't admit this to anyone, and he still wasn't planning on thanking Emmanuel anytime soon, but in a way it had been a relief. The protections his priestess mother had insulated her home with had offered him some respite. Peace of a kind he hadn't felt since he'd left a year ago.

There was no darkness under the Mambo's roof. It was a fact that didn't soothe him as much as he thought it would. It meant he wasn't crazy. It meant there really was something out there. That it hadn't all been in his mind. Had the *djab* escaped his prison and come after him again? Did it want to finish the job? Or was it something more dangerous?

Maybe he should listen to what Emmanuel had been trying to tell him. Maybe he should follow his advice and tell his mother about his experiences this past year. But he hadn't yet. Mainly because he just didn't want to give the irritating bastard the satisfaction.

Instead he was walking around like a bear with a thorn in his paw and no information . . . but at least he had his pride.

And his impeccable sense of sarcasm.

Not knowing was one of the reasons he hadn't wanted to come here tonight. To go out in the world where the shadows dwelt among humanity. Heading back here of all places; the old mansion he and Ben and Michelle used to play behind. The house where they met the youthful specter who, it seemed, had grown up to become a serious pain in his ass.

But he'd had no choice. The Mamas had taken turns glaring and giving him sorrowful looks until he'd agreed to play nice and go spend time with his sister and the rest of the brood. They were argumentative and affectionate. Irreverent and loving. A family. He felt like a fraud among them, like he didn't belong. Their closeness, their obvious warmth for one another, was alien. Strange. He didn't fit, and he was in no shape to carry on a civilized conversation. Especially when the young beauty had turned the conversation to spirit possession as he sat beside his sister and BD, the two people who had seen him at his weakest moment . . . who'd saved him.

He'd come out to the backyard to get away from Celestin's feisty sister, almost daring himself to see something in the darkness. A test, he assured himself. If only to remind him that sparring with a beautiful woman wasn't for someone like him. Not anymore. It was an action Emmanuel had been questioning when Angelique had come upon them.

"I apologize, Angelique. Again. One of the reasons I came out here was to be alone." He eyed Emmanuel meaningfully. "I'm not exactly fit for polite company."

"Hey, progress. You used her name." Emmanuel chuckled.

Her full lips quirked and she shrugged, drawing his gaze back to her silky bare shoulder. He wanted to press his lips against it. He needed help.

"Maybe not. But at least you used my name. Progress."

Emmanuel sent her an odd look as she repeated his sentence nearly word for word. He disappeared suddenly, leaving Gabriel alone with the stubborn Angelique.

Why was she still here? She wasn't getting his hints. Wasn't moving away from him and going back inside. What was her game?

"I know why I had to come, but why are you wasting your evening? You should be out with friends, getting into trouble, enjoying your freedom. Not surrounded by old married couples and a charity case."

She rolled her eyes. " 'Bout done with those age references? It's getting a little stale. Of course, I can wait if you need to get a few more out of your system. Try something about playing in the kiddie pool or grounding me." She pressed her lips together and hummed. "Hmmm. Am I young enough to get a spanking for having such a smart mouth? You could always give that a shot."

He couldn't help it. He smiled. He wasn't used to this kind of banter. She was brazen. Funny. Fearless. None of the socialites or businesswomen in his old circles had her kind of confidence. That special something that shone like a light around her.

And none of them had ever made him this hard.

His smile disappeared and he stepped in close. Close enough to smell her unique scent. It was intoxicating. A small voice in his head reminded him that she was Rousseau's little sister. The Rousseau who was married to *his* sister's best friend. Add more than a decade of difference between their ages and his current mental state, and there was nothing right in what he was thinking.

But that didn't stop him from thinking it.

"Don't tempt me."

Angelique licked her lips, and that quickly, Gabriel couldn't tear his gaze away from her mouth. It curved, gleaming pink and damp and framed by those riveting dimples.

"Do you ever notice how the more people tell you not to do something, the more you want to do it?" she asked.

All the damn time. Her breath skimmed his lips, and he realized she was still leaning back against the tree. He was the one who had moved closer, instinctively. Drawn to her, as he had been from the instant he first saw her.

One taste. Surely that wouldn't damn him any more than he already was. It wouldn't even be the worst thing he'd ever done. But he couldn't give in without trying one more time to do the right thing.

"Feeling rebellious? Bored? You think I'm safe to play at being a bad girl with, here within view of your family and mine. I'd be curious to see how much you think I'll let you tease me. How much I'll let you get away with before I take your dare."

Her response was a low chuckle. A rich, musical sound he wanted to capture. Wanted to hear again. He stilled when she reached up and laid her palm on his chest. Through the linen of his shirt, he could feel her heat. Feel the warmth of her send sharp ripples of desire through his limbs.

It had been a long time since he'd felt like this. Since desire didn't come from desperation. From the need to escape into a willing body. Any willing body. A simple touch and all his attention, all his passion, found a single focus.

Angelique.

And from the twinkle in her doe-brown eyes, she knew it.

Her fingers traced the line of buttons down his shirt to his waist. He lowered his lids, staring at her through his lashes, unwilling to blink. Each muscle in his body was strung tight, waiting to see what she would do next.

She gripped his belt and tugged lightly, bringing him just close enough that he could feel the hardened tips of her full breasts scraping his chest.

"Is this bad girl enough for you? Or should I go on?"

"Jesus." He gripped her wrist and pulled her flush against him, pressing his lips to hers. He couldn't help himself. A saint would have had a difficult time resisting her offer, never mind a man who was used to taking what he wanted and damn the consequences.

Her mouth softened, opened willingly beneath his, and he growled. Her flavor burst on his tongue like summer strawberries. Bright and rich with passion, sweet and delicious. Fucking poetry. But he didn't care. He needed more.

As their tongues tangled, Gabriel dropped her wrist and cupped the voluptuous denim-encased cheeks of her ass. He lifted her up and pressed her against the tree, cradling his cock between her thighs. Heaven.

She wrapped her legs around his waist, her arms curving around his neck, and Gabriel shuddered. There was no hesitance in her embrace. She made no secret of her desire for him. Her fingers twined through the curls at his nape and tugged. Her teeth bit down on his lip, making him moan. She was like living fire in his arms.

The pure, raw honesty of the moment scorched him. Made him want to drink her in. To fill himself up with her until there was no separation. No escape. Until there was no more darkness.

He ground his hips against hers, loving the scrape of the fabric against his flesh. The heat of her. He gripped the elastic fabric of her burgundy top and tugged until the flexible material slipped beneath her breasts, exposing them to his gaze. "I can see the flush on your skin, the nipples that are begging for my touch. My mouth. God, they're perfect, Angelique. Do they taste as good as they look?"

She groaned in response, her head rolling back against the tree as he pressed his lips to one full, creamy breast. His mouth opened wide over the feast, his only thought to taste as much, to take as much, as he could. Sweet and spicy, the hardened nipple tempted him to flick his tongue across it, a temptation he gave in to. His cheeks hollowed as he sucked, the intensity of his need increasing with each thrust of his hips, each tug on her flesh.

She was whimpering when he moved to offer the same treatment to her other breast. He wrapped his lips around her without mercy at the same moment something caught his eye.

Someone.

Emmanuel stood off to the side, gaze locked not on Gabriel, but on Angelique's bare skin. His blue eyes were dark with surprise and unmistakable lust.

In the months since Emmanuel's arrival in his life, the unusual creature had disappeared whenever Gabriel took a woman to his hotel. Why was he here now?

A feeling of possessiveness crashed through him. This was his. This moment. This woman. But that sensation was overcome by the need to make Emmanuel squirm. That, and the fact that he knew he couldn't make himself stop touching Angelique. No matter who was watching.

Gabriel dropped to his knees, taking the breathless Angelique with him, down to the grass behind the large tree that hid them from human eyes.

"What are you doing to me, Gabriel?"

God, he loved the way her voice caught. She was lost in it, already so close to coming her body was quivering beneath his.

She lay on her back, her curls spread out, her blouse at her waist, with the sleeves gathered at her wrists. An offering. A banquet. All for him.

Gabriel glanced up at Emmanuel and smiled before unsnapping Angelique's jeans slowly, tauntingly. "I'm giving you what you wanted when you came out here to look for me. I'm showing you how much better it is to be bad."

He jerked his chin toward the house. "And you are being bad, aren't you, Angelique? That house full of people would never guess in a million years how bad you want to be. That you let me do this—" His breath came out in a low, shaky prayer as he tugged the denim down over her bent knees, revealing the lacy red thong barely covering her sex. "Oh, that's pretty. That you'd let me do more than this. Anything. Because you crave it as much as I do, don't you?"

Angelique's eyes were wide, her teeth digging into her lower lip as she stared at him. Gabriel knew Emmanuel had fallen to his knees as well, as caught up as he was in the sensual vision on the grass.

When she didn't answer, Gabriel slid one hand between her legs, his trembling fingers tracing the damp lace, loving how wet she was.

"I think you do, Angelique. You crave the risk. The excitement. I think you were one of those girls who sat next to a boy in the dark movie theater, your thighs pressing together as you imagined him touching you, slipping his hand up your dress and down your pretty panties. Fucking you with his fingers while the people around you stared at the screen, oblivious. But that would have been the most exciting part, wouldn't it? The fact that they could look up at any moment and see you, your legs spread, your hips thrusting . . ."

Gabriel's voice was guttural, his throat tight, as he echoed his words with his fingers. They were inside her. She was tight. So hot she soaked him as he pushed one, then two, of his thick, callused fingers inside her velvet sheath.

His cock was so hard it hurt. And he felt it again. Like he needed more of her. More of her light. More of her passion. He wanted to drown in her. What was it about this woman that worked him into this kind of frenzy?

She lifted her hips, forcing his fingers deep, and he heard Emmanuel's heartfelt groan. "God help me."

Gabriel could have echoed the sentiment. Only he knew it would have been a hollow prayer. He could pretend all he liked . . . but he didn't want to escape. Not from this.

The thought should have sent him far away. Instead, he

lifted her legs and bent down until his teeth were snagging on the ruby-red lace that concealed her. The shredding sound as the weblike underwear dissolved made him smile.

She wasn't the only one who could be bad. Hell, Gabriel had written the book on it.

CHAPTER 3

WHAT IN THE NAME OF SWEET HOLY HEAVEN HAD SHE GOT-
ten herself into? Talk about the kiddie pool. She'd just jumped
into the deep end without knowing how to swim.

She'd known pleasure. She'd known passion. But it was like
comparing a firecracker to a nuclear explosion. Angelique realized as soon as Gabriel started kissing her that she was way out
of her league.

Now she was on her back on the ground with her pants
down, Gabriel's head between her thighs, and family within
shouting distance.

And she couldn't care less.

The pictures he'd drawn in her mind with that husky whisper were shocking. Scandalous. Had she ever wondered what it

would be like, having someone watch her? Now it was all she could think of.

The fantasy was so strong she opened her eyes, sure she would find a man watching from the darkness. A man wanting to touch her. Wanting his tongue, instead of Gabriel's, gliding along the lips of her sex, wanting to suck her clit while his fingers plunged deep inside her.

For an instant she thought she saw . . . and then her eyes blurred with pleasure. She was coming. So hard the power of it pulled her off the grass. Her back arched and her teeth bit into her hand to stop her screams.

But he was nowhere near done. Her skin was still tingling from her orgasm, every inch scalded by his touch, and a lightning storm of energy and passion zapped along her nerve endings as he silently demanded more with his mouth. His fingers. His tongue.

She could almost feel it. She was dizzy. Light-headed. It was the strangest sensation, as though he was consuming her down to her soul. Every bit of her being drawn into him. This was more than desire. More than lust. But whatever it was, she didn't care right now. She just didn't want it to end.

His tongue curled inside her sex, vibrating with his moan as though he loved the taste of her. Couldn't get enough.

Her hands reached down to sift through his hair again, loving the softness of it, the velvet waves curling around her fingers—the only thing about Gabriel that wasn't rough and hard. The only thing she had to hang on to as he brought her back to the edge of madness with a few firm thrusts of his fingers.

His other hand reached up to grip one of her wrists, tugging her hand out of his hair and guiding it to her breast. She looked down at his green eyes, dark and sparkling like jewels, his intent clear.

He wanted to watch as she touched herself.

Angelique licked her lips, unable to stop them from curving up. Her other hand lifted to join the first and she cupped the heavy globes of her breasts, presenting them to him like an offering.

He gently bit the sensitive flesh of her sex in approval, and she shivered.

She squeezed her nipples between her fingers, a tight twist that made her thighs quiver and his gaze narrow. She did it again. *Yes*. She liked that. Liked the zap of pain, the flash of pleasure that followed in a rush behind it.

He did, too. But she knew what he would like even more.

She pressed her breasts together and lifted her head off the grass, her tongue darting out to lick one nipple, then the other.

Gabriel lifted his mouth and growled. "Again."

Angelique obeyed. She moaned in disappointment when he rose to his knees, leaving her wanting. She was so close to coming again. So close to falling over that cliff that was quickly becoming her addiction. But one look at his expression and she knew he wasn't going anywhere. His fingers, still damp with her arousal, reached down to close over the brass button of his pants. The sound of his zipper sent a shudder through her. This was really happening. Right here. Right now.

Oh God.

"Oh—um—well, shit."

The unfortunately familiar female voice sent Angelique and Gabriel scrambling away from each other. She cursed silently as her sluggish hands readjusted her blouse, covering her breasts.

Her jeans and the remnants of her thong were a bit more difficult of a proposition.

She looked up at Gabriel, thankful that he'd moved to stand between her and Bethany as she got to her feet and hopped herself back into her jeans. She shoved a scrap of red lace into her pocket and tried to focus on the hushed conversation going on in front of her.

Bethany sounded strained. "They noticed Angelique was gone. We told them we saw her head toward the front door, and that we thought you'd gone home."

"I appreciate the circumspection." Gabriel sounded strange.

Angelique peered around his broad shoulders to study his face. Emotionless. Almost cold. Could he turn it off so quickly, then? She'd never been that good at hiding her emotions, and right now she was a tangled mass of nerves—not to mention frustration, embarrassment, and unbelievable arousal.

Bethany sent her a sympathetic glance just as her husband appeared behind her.

BD raised one elegant eyebrow as he took in the situation. He snared Angelique's gaze, one side of his mouth quirking upward. "Yes. You are definitely my favorite Rousseau."

Bethany dug her elbow into his ribs and he winced. "What? You didn't marry a puritan, Blue Eyes. And it's not as if you don't enjoy a touch of risk now and then. I distinctly remember a certain store's dressing roo—oomph!"

Angelique tried to hide her smile when Bethany whirled around and covered her husband's mouth with her hand. "Public displays of affection aren't the issue here, okay? And keep your voice down."

Understanding dawned in BD's amber eyes and he tugged Bethany's hand away from his mouth, kissing it apologetically. "The players and not the game. I see. And you're right as usual, my love. Rousseau is more the punch first, think later sort. Especially when it comes to things he can't explain. Like me." He smiled, lost in a memory. "But he usually comes around."

Angelique shook her head. Yes, she might have chosen a more secluded spot, if she'd known how well and truly lost to Gabriel's touch she'd become. But she wasn't sorry it happened. And she wasn't going to act like a toddler with a hand in the cookie jar. "Well, you may see it, but I don't. What I choose to do is exactly that. My choice. My brother needs to get used to that."

She placed her hand on Gabriel's arm and his muscles tensed. He backed away from her and ran a hand through his hair. "It isn't about you at all, Angelique. It's about me."

He refused to look at her, to look at any of them, as he continued to back farther away. She watched his gaze dart around the yard, peering through the shadows. "I shouldn't be here. I have to go. Forgive me."

She stood beside the tree and watched him disappear around

one side of the rambling old mansion just as her brother and Ben appeared from the other.

Son of a bitch. What was wrong with that man? She knew it wasn't fear of Celestin that sent him racing off into the night. No. Something else was going on.

Or are you just fooling yourself because you want him?

Maybe, she admitted silently. But she didn't think so. She wasn't sure how she knew, but she did. Gabriel's responses to her had been real. The chemistry she'd been feeling between them was real. And so volatile it had overwhelmed her.

A part of Angelique was still reeling from the experience. She'd come alive for the first time in a way she could hardly explain. Her miniature obsession with the scowling bad boy had taken an unexpected turn. Now that she knew what he could do to her body with a single touch . . .

She just had to find out what he—what *everyone*—was hiding from her about him. Now more than ever.

Bethany's words fell right in line with her plan. "Babe, could you distract the boys and tell Michelle and Allegra we'll be back in a few minutes, please? I think we need to have a girl talk."

BD bowed quickly and winked at the women. "For you? Anything." He raised his voice and headed toward the two scowling men who'd reached the gazebo. "Rousseau, Ben, did I ever tell you about the time I was called to help a certain senator with a penchant for, shall we say, letting someone else have the *reins*?"

Bethany sighed and sat down beside the tree, where Angelique had been on her back only moments before. "I'm exhausted. Come on, have a seat."

She sat down, studying the woman who was studying her. Noticing the evidence that Angelique could feel all over her face. The heat and redness on her cheeks and neck from Gabriel's stubble. The swollen lips. She braced herself for the imminent interrogation.

"What do you want to know?"

Angelique frowned. "Huh?"

Bethany lifted one shoulder. "We have a couple of choices here. Number one, I could let Michelle talk to you. But if past experience is anything to go by—and trust me, it is—she'll warn you to stay away from Gabriel. She's protective; it's just her way. And she's already worried about her brother."

Angelique figured as much. She wrapped her arms around her knees and sighed. "What are our other choices?"

"We could let *your* brother see the way you look right now and step aside while he pummels Gabriel into a handsome pile of goo, but I don't think any of us wants that." Bethany twirled a broken twig between her fingers. "Or . . . I could just satisfy your curiosity about him, and let you make your own decisions."

Angelique reached out and squeezed Bethany's hand. "That's the nicest choice anyone has ever given me."

"Trust me, I know how you feel." Bethany grinned. "You asked what happened last year? Well, other than Allegra loving your brother so much that she offered a Loa a gift he

49

couldn't refuse to free him, and me discovering said Loa was my reincarnated lover who was waiting for a second chance with me . . ." She stopped at Angelique's confused expression and laughed. "*You* wanted to know. Allegra's writing another story about them. I mean us. Marcel and Isabel. It's confusing. I'll tell you about it sometime, but I think you wanted to know about what happened to Gabriel."

Angelique nodded, her eyes wide. "Yes. But later, I definitely want to know about Marcel and Isabel."

Bethany's smile disappeared. "You know about Michelle's ability to see ghosts. What you don't know is that there was a time when she tried not to. Back when we first met. Michelle came back to New Orleans because she was faced with something she couldn't avoid. A violent spirit who liked being noticed almost as much as he enjoyed inflicting pain."

"Oh my."

But Bethany wasn't done. "It followed her back home. It waited. And when Gabriel showed up out of the blue, having just discovered most of his life was one mean, hurtful lie . . . the spirit possessed him to try and hurt his sister. And it very nearly succeeded."

Angelique placed her fingers at her temple and rubbed. She felt like she'd jumped into this conversation in the middle. Or into a strange piece of fiction. If zombies suddenly sprang out from behind the gazebo, she wouldn't be surprised.

"So he was possessed? But how? I mean, doesn't he have abilities that protect him? Like Michelle's?"

Bethany shook her head. "I don't think so. Michelle had

her gift for as long as she could remember, but Gabriel never showed any signs." She leaned her head back against the tree, lost in thought. "Michelle told me they were eight when his father took him away to Italy. That she found out after the attack about the priests and all the beatings he suffered to make sure he wasn't like her. Really horrible stuff. I imagine that kind of abuse would knock the magic out of anybody."

Or the hope. Angelique ached for him. The story explained the stark loneliness in his eyes. The vulnerability that he covered up with his gruff demeanor.

"What about this last year? Why did he leave?"

Bethany lifted one dark brow. "Would *you* want to stay? He tried. Mambo Toussaint told me he stayed up several nights reading all the letters his sister had written to him through the years. The ones his father had sent back unopened. He spent a little time with his mother, looking at some old pictures and letting her feed him, but after a month or two he took off. All we know is he didn't go back to Italy. And that he seems to be, well, worse than when he left."

Bethany bit her lip, as if holding something back.

"You may as well tell her, my darling. You've given her everything else."

Bethany looked up at her husband and wrinkled her nose. "What part of *girl talk* don't you understand, Sugar Cakes?"

BD knelt down beside them, an offended expression crossing his stunning features. "I know all about this girl talk of which you speak. Sometimes it leads to girl pillow fights, girl kissing—" He laughed when Bethany swatted his arm half-

51

heartedly and glanced at Angelique. "There is something in the air around him. Something strange. But our Michelle can't see it with her vision. And from what Benjamin just told me, when he shook Gabriel's hand he sensed it as well. Something just out of reach. Something with him, blocked from both of them. It scares them. For Gabriel's sake, and everyone else's."

Angelique shivered.

Something *with* him? Maybe that was what he was talking to when she found him—had it been little more than an hour ago?

It was hard to wrap her mind around. Or her emotions. She was angry for the little boy who'd been torn from his mother and abused. Horrified over the terrifying scenario of possession Bethany had described. And still curious about the mystery surrounding him. Where had he been? What had happened to him? And why was he back?

"Fate. Destiny."

Angelique and Bethany both stared at BD in question.

"The Marassa Twins wouldn't leave the brother of a *bon ange* out in the darkness alone. Whether they gave him gifts or not. Maybe they're giving him a chance to really find his way back home. Maybe now was exactly the right time."

"Marassa Twins?"

Bethany let BD pull her closer as she answered. "The Loa that gave Michelle her gift. The ones that watch over twins, and sometimes grant them special abilities."

Angelique tilted her head. "See, that doesn't make any sense. That they would only give *her* special abilities. Has anyone ever asked him?" Not that she really knew anything about the whims or personalities of voodoo spirits, but that didn't seem very fair.

What if Gabriel did, after all, have some kind of ability that made Michelle and Ben, both powerful in their own right, nervous?

What if it was that ability that was making her act this way? Would that explain her inability to think of anything else? Her reaction to him, despite his arrogance?

She reached up to touch the small cross around her neck, knowing logically that there was no bad juju involved in her attraction. But it was definitely a weakness. More than just wanting him, now that she knew a little more about him, she wished she could take away his pain. Wished she could fix it. But this wasn't a rotting bridge or a leaky dam. This might be something too big for her to handle.

Maybe she *should* stay away from Gabriel.

Angelique thought about the thrill she'd gotten when she'd made him smile. The passion that changed his green eyes from hunted to hauntingly beautiful. No, she wasn't sure she was ready to let her obsession with Gabriel go just yet. There were still too many unanswered questions.

And unsatisfied desires.

She looked up at BD to find him watching her with an expression of interest and delight. "Scared yet?"

CHAPTER 4

WALKING HOME WAS NOT THE BEST IDEA HE'D EVER HAD.
Why hadn't he taken a taxi or one of those damn streetcars?
He wasn't thinking logically. And it was all her fault.

Gabriel passed by several bars where the music and people
overflowed out onto the street in colorful waves of sexuality
and laughter. Distraction waited with open arms to embrace
him, to bring him oblivion. One way or another.

It wasn't enough anymore. Not now. He slid his tongue
along the roof of his mouth. Her taste filled his senses. The
scent of her arousal lingered around him, keeping his cock rock
hard and his mind filled with images of her body spread out
beneath him.

He'd felt more than lust when he touched her. And when

she came . . . Gabriel had felt charged. Energized. As if he could take on anything. Even the man who appeared beside him, looking decidedly out of sorts.

"Hey, Manny," he teased, "have fun tonight?"

Emmanuel shoved his hands in the pockets of his long trench coat and frowned. "Don't call me that. And I could ask the same of you, couldn't I? I didn't bring you back here to cause a family feud by fiddling with Rousseau's baby sister."

Gabriel smirked. "I know, I know. You're on a very mysterious mission to be my own personal Peeping Tom. Do your bosses know what you do with your downtime? Or maybe you want to be the one doing the fiddling. Since I'm not sure what you are, I don't know—can you even do that kind of thing?"

"Smart-ass." Emmanuel sounded agitated. "I'll apologize if you want. I didn't realize you would be . . . It won't happen again."

"I can't blame you." Gabriel was no longer smiling. "I didn't realize it, either." And he would be wise to make sure it didn't happen again. Though every inch of him apart from his brain rejected that thought. "She's a force of nature, isn't she?"

"You don't even know what you actually did to her. What you could do."

What he did to her? "What are you talking about now? I've done nothing to her."

Except make her angry. Make her come. And then leave her to deal with the uncomfortable fallout alone because he thought he saw something moving in the shadows.

He was a piece of work.

Emmanuel scuffed a pebble with his boot. "If you'd listened to me and talked to the Mambo about what you've been experiencing, you wouldn't need to ask me that. I'm here to make sure you don't lose your way. Your mother can help you."

Gabriel stopped down the dark side street that was the shortcut home. "This is bullshit. I don't give a *flying fuck* what you are, but just what the hell is your purpose here? All you've done so far is make dire predictions and harass me."

"I'm trying to protect you from—"

"Losing myself to the darkness," Gabriel snarled. "So you keep saying. It's nothing I haven't heard before. But what you don't understand is if there *is* a darkness coming for me, the last thing I want to do is bring my mother into this. Don't you get it? You were alive once; you had a family. Don't you fucking get it?"

Gabriel remembered the stories Michelle had told him when they were young. The ghost child whose family had lived in the big white house a century before. Emmanuel's memories of his beautiful sister. He should know all about protecting family.

Gabriel scrubbed his face with his hands, feeling the stubble scrape his palms. "I'm not so blind that I can't see I've caused her enough suffering. All of them. Can't you just tell me what's going on?"

Emmanuel placed a hand on his shoulder. It wasn't solid, but Gabriel sensed it like a cool, steady breeze. "You think I don't understand? I do. It would be easier to just tell you everything. Gabe, I—" He stopped speaking suddenly, his body tensed. Alert. "I wasn't expecting this. Maybe the powers that be would rather show than tell."

"What's that supposed to mean? What powers that be?"

"Check this fool out. Talkin' to himself. Crazy, drunk, or just plain stupid; either way, you picked the wrong street tonight."

Gabriel eyed the group of five young toughs who were spreading out in front of him. Twentysomethings covered in tattoos and attitude, their aggressive posturing unmistakable.

Also unmistakable was the darkness that was coalescing around them. Clearer than he'd ever seen it. Was it getting stronger?

Emmanuel spoke beside him, as if answering his thoughts. "You've sobered up. That gives you a little more control. Use it."

Use it? Use what?

The men stepped closer, their animosity increasing as the energy swirled around them. "Looks like he's too stupid to talk. I was hoping for more of a challenge, but maybe quick and dirty is better. Be home in time to watch my shows."

What was it? He barely heard the kids posturing as he studied the shadows around him. It wasn't a *djab*. This close he could sense the difference. That was a relief, he supposed, though the only one he could find in the situation.

Sooty darkness that was more absence of light than form. It was also less focused, less sentient, than the spirit he'd been taken over by, but no less threatening.

It appeared to gravitate toward the most confrontational men in the group like a plant reaching for the sun. But was it influencing those emotions, causing them, or just drawn to them?

He knew the instant it noticed him. Like a predator sensing it was being watched, it stilled and seemed to turn in his direction.

Maybe that bastard, Father Leon, was right, and evil recognized him as one of its own. That familiar tension, the heaviness he'd come to associate with the shadows, settled around him as the darkness drew closer. It wanted to control him. To take him over.

Emmanuel's voice, sounding far away, was urgent. "Focus, Gabriel. Use it; don't let it use you. Shit, you aren't ready for this."

A haze covered his eyes and he felt his upper lip curl in an ugly sneer. "Fuck you. I can handle these punks with my eyes closed. If you don't have anything constructive to say, just shut the hell up."

The chorus of disbelieving voices made Gabriel realize he'd spoken aloud. They thought he was talking to them.

"Great."

The largest of the five shook his head, and Gabriel noticed the shadows tangling like razor-sharp vines around this thug in particular. He could feel them around his own body, too, seeping into his flesh, creeping through his veins like a dark, sizzling poison.

The group's leader held out his hands, bringing Gabriel's attention back to him. "See? Some people just don't know how this game works. Now I have to let the boys take turns bouncing your head off the sidewalk. But only after I get mine."

The first punch came quick and knocked him to his knees.

What the hell? He did a quick internal inventory. Nothing was broken. This time.

It was a damn shame he wasn't drinking anymore. The fights he'd been getting into for the past year hurt a lot less when he'd been drinking.

While the men laughed around him, he looked up at Emmanuel. "I assume you'll be no fucking help at all, will you?"

Emmanuel winced, but shook his head. "Not this time. I'm sorry, Gabe. I wish I could knock that bastard out for you, but I'm not supposed to interfere unless your life is in danger. I can tell you this isn't a possession. What you're seeing isn't out of their control or yours. You have more power here than you know."

"Yeah. That's readily apparent." He stumbled to his feet, the weight of the strange darkness heavy around him and the power of that last punch making his limbs leaden and sluggish.

Use it? Even if he could find a way to use this whatever-it-was to his advantage, he wouldn't want to. If he did, he'd be no better than these angry punks. No better than the *djab* who'd stalked his sister, the piously pugilistic Father Leon, or any of the other priests who'd taken delight in punishing him for his sins. He would be beyond redemption.

A part of him was afraid that was a foregone conclusion regardless.

"You want some more?" The leader posed for his cheering friends and flexed. "I can do this all night."

Before Gabriel could brace himself, the next punch split his lip, the coppery taste of blood replacing Angelique's essence.

"You're beginning to piss me off," Gabriel growled. "Why don't you all run back home and have your mommies teach you some manners, eh? And stop playing all those violent video games. They're giving you delusions of grandeur."

He could tell his quips didn't go over well. It certainly hadn't done anything to ease the tension. The small group converged on him, anger at his insult burning like stinging embers in their eyes.

If he woke up from this, he would know that somebody up there liked him—or just really enjoyed watching him suffer. If he didn't . . . An image of Angelique pressing her delicious breasts together, her tongue curling around the crest of one perfect nipple, filled his vision.

It was a good thought to die to.

A quiet voice in his head had another theory. *Maybe, just maybe, it's a good thought to live for.*

Either way, it was the last one he had before he lost consciousness. Again.

"DAMN, YOU ARE A SAD-LOOKING SIGHT, BOY. CALL THE Mambo now, *cher*. Tell her we found her son, and he'll be staying with us for the night. I don't think she needs to know anything else right now."

Gabriel groaned, opening one heavy eyelid to find BD sitting beside him. He was naked in a strange bedroom, and he could see the pale face of Michelle's friend Bethany hovering over her husband's shoulder, a cell phone to her ear.

He was still alive. In their house. It was an oddly comforting realization. His mother didn't need to see him like this again. And BD? BD had seen him in his darkest hour. He'd been there with Michelle, literally the spirit inside her who'd dragged the *djab* out of Gabriel's body and sent it into the void last year before the Loa had become human.

Somehow the fact that he was here made perfect sense. But he still wasn't sure how that miracle had come about.

"H-how?"

The ex-Loa lifted his eyebrows. "I was just about to ask you the same thing, *mon ami*. How, by Legba's walking stick, did you manage to do so much damage in one night?"

"Me?" Gabriel tried to sit up, swearing as his ribs protested painfully. "I was just walking home. Minding my own business. I was attacked by—"

"Five men. Brutes, all of them, I know." BD was nodding. "That's what the littlest one said. Well, not in so many words. He was too scared to make much sense, but who could blame him, yes?"

Scared? Gabriel took a few deep breaths, hoping a bit more oxygen to his brain would help him think past the aches in his body and make sense of the conversation. "I don't know what you're talking about, but whatever you did, thank you. Once again, you saved my life. I'm not sure how I got out of this last one intact."

He wiggled his toes and fingers. They hurt, too, but at least they were moving. Yes. Intact. Unbelievable.

BD shrugged. "I did nothing. It was the strangest thing. We

were on our way home from Adair's house—talking about you, by the way—and my wife heard a voice in her ear telling us where to find you." He smiled at Gabriel's expression of disbelief. "My wife, having never heard a disembodied voice before, decided it would be best to obey. And I make it a rule never to argue with my wife. Imagine our surprise when we find you in the center of a pile of bodies, all alive, but most in the same shape as you are now."

Gabriel opened his mouth to deny it, but BD raised his voice, his hands moving expansively as he continued. "Imagine our *increased* surprise when one of them begins to spin a tale about the easy tourist mark who became a horrifying wild man with angry black eyes and iron fists."

BD tapped his chin thoughtfully, his eyes sparkling. "It's sure to become an urban myth. Perhaps a morality tale that will, at the very least, keep those particular young men out of trouble. For a while."

Gabriel lowered his head gingerly back to the pillow and closed his eyes. "You could be speaking Japanese backward with a lisp and I'd be able to piece together what you're talking about more clearly than I can now. Maybe I have a concussion."

"Oh, he's funny. No one told me he was funny." Bethany, apparently off the phone now, reappeared beside the bed.

Gabriel's lips twitched and he peered at her through his lashes. "Ouch."

She smiled. "Sorry. Any idea why I heard a voice telling me where to find my best friend's brother?"

BD laughed. "Do you see why I love her? She's as direct as

she is sexy." He wrapped one arm around her waist and tugged her against him, lifting her shirt and kissing her stomach before she batted him away. She sent an apologetic glance to Gabriel, but there was no need. BD made his own rules, even without his previous abilities.

The man sent Gabriel a wink. "How about we let him rest and heal for now, Blue Eyes? I see you're dying of curiosity, as am I. Who is this man who seduced Rousseau's sister and transformed into a Crescent City vigilante all in one night?" He stood and embraced his wife. "I know how hard it will be for you to restrain yourself from getting answers, but if you give me a chance, I will do my best to distract you until morning."

Bethany bit her upper lip, as though considering his offer. "Your best, huh?"

BD slid a palm down to cup her hip, uncaring or no longer aware of his audience. "Yes. I'll even do that one thing you love so much. Where I take your legs and—"

Bethany placed a finger against his lips, stopping his words. But she couldn't quite hide the expression of arousal and interest.

The sensual intimacy of the look they shared was so un-apologetically loving, so honestly sexual, that it tore the breath from Gabriel's lungs.

He closed his eyes again, focusing on slowing his breathing so they would think he'd fallen asleep. He didn't want to see any more of this.

He remembered hearing his mother tell him about BD and Bethany's unique love story. How they'd found each other with the help of the voodoo spirits. A match made in heaven, with Papa Legba and the Ghede family's blessing.

He'd been told by his teachers that his mother worshipped demons. But he hadn't learned about matchmaking demons in catechism. Evil didn't care about the happiness of a single man and woman. Evil didn't create what Gabriel saw between Bethany and BD.

Michelle and Ben were like that, too. What they felt for each other was so clear for the world to see, it was almost painful to watch.

Was that love, then?

His father had married again and again, and with each new woman he became a new man. His last wife, the hippie Wiccan, was the reason behind his father's sudden change of heart. When he'd told Gabriel that he'd lied, that it had been his decision, not his mother's, to take their son away . . . it had been a shock to Gabriel's system.

But his father's spiritual epiphany had been more about pleasing his latest conquest than out of any concern for his son. Not love, just weakness.

Women had professed to love Gabriel often enough through the years, women who were drawn to his family's money or the air of authority he'd always had around him, but he didn't think he'd ever truly seen it before. Not what he was seeing now.

He heard their whispers, the footsteps heading toward the bedroom door, and the click as it shut behind them. He breathed a sigh of relief. He needed time to think about what had happened tonight.

Black-eyed, ironfisted wild man? Was that what BD had said? Surely he hadn't been referring to him. The last thing Gabriel had remembered, he was getting his ass kicked, with that mysterious darkness swirling around him, and Angelique on his mind. He hadn't seen the monster BD had described.

Had he become one?

Emmanuel had said it wasn't possession, but if not that, then what? And where had it come from? It seemed to have been dragged out from corner shadows when the group of would-be attackers surrounded him.

Sure, this time he'd been paying attention, but he still had no idea what the darkness was or why it was drawn to him. Emmanuel, no matter what he said he wanted to do, was *not* helping.

Would BD know the answers? Maybe that was why his friendly ghost-but-not-a-ghost had whispered in Bethany's ear the way Gabriel believed he had. If BD really did have some knowledge about this, he had only two important questions.

What exactly was he becoming? And how could he make it stop?

He was wondering if he had enough strength to get up and see if they had anything to eat when a soft female moan drifted through the wall.

"Perfect," he mumbled. He was the bruised and battered houseguest of a man with a legendary sexual appetite and his willing wife. You'd think they would have planned ahead and invested in thicker walls.

Another moan, this one louder, had Gabriel gritting his teeth. Now he was the voyeur. Only, in his mind, it wasn't Bethany's pleasure he was hearing.

Angelique had made a sound just like that when he'd rocked her against that tree. When he'd laid her on the ground and slipped his fingers inside her tight, wet heat. Sweet sounds. Greedy sounds. He wanted to hear them again.

His fist clenched around the sheet covering him, the aches and pains in his body doing nothing to hinder the rush of blood and need flowing directly to his cock.

God, he wanted her. More than he'd imagined possible. One taste wasn't enough. Despite all the logic that told him he should stay as far away from her as humanly possible—for her safety and his—it hadn't been enough.

He wanted her naked beneath him. On top of him. In a bed, against a tree—he didn't care. He *needed* to be inside her. He needed what only she could give him.

In his mind he saw her walk into the room. So damn sexy. And she knew it. She smiled coyly at him and her dimples deepened. Dimples he wanted to lick.

Her breasts were flushed with desire, her hips swaying to a music only she could hear as she walked toward him wearing nothing but a red lace thong.

Gabriel moaned, one hand slipping beneath the sheets to grip his erection. The only part of him that hadn't been hurting . . . until now.

His fantasy Angelique's smile turned into a moue of concern, her hand reaching out to skim along his calf and up to his thigh. When she reached his hip he held his breath, but she hesitated.

"Yes, touch me. You won't hurt me. I've been dying to feel your hands on me."

His dream girl didn't disappoint. She dragged the sheet slowly off his body, revealing his bruised torso, licking her lips at the first sight of his arousal.

He wanted that, too. Wanted her mouth on him. Those sweet berry lips. His fist tightened as he thought about how soft they'd be on his skin.

Angelique read his mind. Kneeling on the bed, the curve of her ass making his mouth water as she bent to wrap her lips around the head of his erection.

She moaned and Gabriel lifted his hips, needing more. Just. A little more.

"Please." She had him begging. But she held her mouth just out of reach, teasing and tempting him, even in his own damn fantasy. "Angelique, baby, I need . . ."

She laughed, that musical sound he remembered, and cupped her breasts in her hands. He looked down to see her slipping his cock between the two velvet globes and growled. "Jesus."

Yes.

His bad, brazen angel. She knew just what he wanted. What he needed. The bed beneath him squeaked and his heart was pounding loud in his ears. Passion pulsed through his body, tearing through him, pulling a harsh groan out of his tight throat as he came.

He could see his arousal coating her breasts, watching it glisten on her skin. He wanted to clean her with his tongue. Start all over again. But he was too tired, his body demanding rest.

He fell asleep to the image of her smiling, the light around her keeping all the shadows at bay.

CHAPTER 5

ANGELIQUE STIRRED HER SODA ABSENTLY WITH A STRAW, lost in thought. The soulful jazz singer that was playing piano on the stage behind her seemed to have her number. She'd always loved this bar. It was small and cozy, and the musicians never disappointed. Almost never. Tonight, however, the headliner was singing one song after another about the man she couldn't get out of her mind, the man who got away, or the man who didn't know she existed in the first place.

The man who kissed her against a tree, made her come, and then disappeared.

Okay, that wasn't a song, but it should be. Maybe she should suggest it.

It had been five days, nearly six, since she'd seen him. She was trying to be patient, but it was harder than that month she'd attempted giving up chocolate. And she really loved chocolate.

After her talk with Bethany last week, she'd decided to take a few days to cool off. To take in what had happened between her and Gabriel. Try to piece together what she'd learned.

She'd wanted him to notice her. And boy, had he ever. The effect had been earthshaking.

Chasing after Gabriel was more than a challenge. The way he made her feel, it could be downright dangerous. Partly because the man was obviously struggling through something more complicated than simple lust. After what she'd heard, she could hardly blame him for his attitude. She'd probably be pissed off at the world, too, if she'd grown up the way he had.

And still she wanted him.

A small—okay, large—part of her had been hoping he would come to her apartment and demand they finish what they'd started the other night. The way he did each night in her dreams.

She closed her eyes and took a deep breath. Just thinking about what he'd done to her in those dreams made her body heat. Sent a fine tremor along her limbs. She was no prude, but she'd had no idea her imagination was that inventive. Why was she so drawn to him?

"Rum."

Angelique looked up at the sound of the deep, male voice. A man with bruises along his jaw and bloodshot eyes was standing at the bar beside her. He was massive. Taller and broader than her brother, and that was saying something. His skin was flushed and his lips had a cruel, knowing curve. When the bartender set a glass in front of him, he pushed it away. "Bring the bottle."

She squirmed. One of those. She glanced back down at her drink, hoping he'd take the hint.

He didn't. "You mooning over a man, girl? You should join me for a drink. It dulls the pain."

"No, thank you." *Please go away*, she shouted mentally. The last thing she needed was to spend the evening dodging a drunk's advances. Especially one who felt so . . . violent. Off-putting.

"He isn't worth it. I can tell. You are too young and pretty to take on someone else's troubles and make them your own."

The female echo of, "Geaux Tigers!" made Angelique beam with relief. She twirled around on her barstool to face the two women beaming behind her. They were finally here.

She stood and shrugged at the man. "Thanks, but I already have a date."

Her friends spread their arms wide, pulling her in for a hug, and she laughed. She'd missed them more than she'd realized.

"You made it."

"Hello? Remember us? 'Kelly and Ive, always come, never leave'? Did you think we *wouldn't* find a way to get here? Especially after those last few e-mails. So mysterious."

Ive grinned at Kelly's words, nodding. "Exactly. We both read your sister-in-law's book, by the way. Woo, *bebe*, was it *good*. Every last filthy, raunchy page. Now we're dying of curiosity. Is he real? Or have you been pulling our legs?"

Angelique guided them to an open table in the back, ignoring the chuckling bartender who'd overheard them. She could only hope they hadn't given that strange man any ideas. "Shh, yes, he's real. And very married to a fantastic woman."

Kelly slid into the small booth, a humorous pout on her lips. "Well, damn. I was all set for a New Orleans Bone Daddy hunt."

Angelique looked at the two of them and felt herself relaxing. This was exactly what she needed. Ive and Kelly had been her roommates since her first year in college. They'd been together through every cram session, every celebration, and more than a few ice cream runs and crying jags.

They were close. Especially those two. Ive had another year until she was done with pre-med, so Kelly had decided to stay in Baton Rouge and work instead of heading back home to Chicago so they could keep the small apartment they had lived in for the last few years. Well, that was the reason she gave, but Angelique knew there was more to it than that. Kelly didn't want to go home. Not yet. It was something else the three of them had always had in common.

Kelly popped back up to order drinks at the bar, and Ive crossed her arms, eyeing Angelique sternly. "Something's wrong."

"Nothing's wrong," Angelique assured her friend. "A lot more family togetherness than I'm used to, but other than that everything is fine."

Ive shook her head. "Uh-huh, keep it up, Angelique, and maybe, eventually, I'll believe you. The way you could eventually believe Kelly doesn't like to sing and I can resist a shoe sale."

"No spilling any secrets without me." Kelly handed Ive a frozen margarita and sat back down, rubbing her hands together in delight. "Has she decided to take that job and move back in with us yet? Because we would be willing to sacrifice the extra bathroom space in a heartbeat. Or does this have to do with the mysterious man thing? There's so much to talk about. It's been so long since we've had an in-person gossip session."

Angelique made a face. "It's been a few months. Besides, I tell you everything. I could be killed by the magical voodoo police for all the beans I've spilled."

Kelly's eyebrows rose and she gasped. "They have voodoo police?"

Ive and Angelique looked at each other and burst out laughing. Kelly threw a napkin at them. "Well, how am I supposed to know? I'm a Yankee. We don't have magic up North. Better pizza, yes, but no magic."

Ive thickened her usually hidden Cajun accent and patted Kelly's hand. "Dere, dere, *cher*. We gunna get you fixed up wid a nice Nawlins prince. He gunna sex the Yank right outta you, yeah, you right."

"Stop; I can't breathe." Angelique was laughing so hard at Ive's words and Kelly's hopeful expression that tears were spilling down her cheeks.

Ive chuckled. "I'll only stop if you tell us about your man. The one you are so carefully *not* talking about."

The only problem with friends like these was they knew you too well. But wasn't that why she'd suggested they get together when they told her they were coming to New Orleans for the weekend? She needed to talk to someone. Trouble was, in this town, everyone she knew was related to her by blood, marriage, or circumstance. And none of them wanted to hear about her Gabriel fixation.

Her friends had gone through a few margaritas by the time she finished telling them about the last two weeks. And they were looking at her like she'd grown a second head.

Kelly's brow was furrowed when she finally spoke. "I don't know, Angelique, hon. He sounds like he needs a giant baseball bat to the head to me. *I* may gravitate toward commitment-phobes, but you've never had to chase a man in your life. Is he blind?"

Angelique placed her elbow on the table, chin in her hand, and sighed. "It is new territory, I'll admit. But not unheard of. Besides, there's something about him."

"He's about trouble, and we all need a bit of trouble in our lives every once in a while." Ive gave her an understanding hug. "We trust your instincts, hon. But if he hurts you, we'll revisit that baseball bat idea. I know a place in the bayou where his body will never be found."

Angelique smiled gratefully. "I love you guys."

Kelly sniffed. "We know you do. Now, I refuse to have another drink unless you join us, lightweight. You don't want to be a bad hostess in your own city, do you?"

Angelique banged the tabletop. "Absolutely not. Margaritas all 'round."

Ive shook her head. "No. I'm afraid we're well past our margarita moment. For what we have planned? We need something a little stronger. And you need something a lot stronger."

"What do you mean, what you have planned?"

"Never you mind. Just do exactly what we say, and no one gets hurt." The look in Ive's eyes was familiar. Too familiar.

Angelique chuckled. "I love it when you get all bossy, Dr. Ive. But whenever you make plans, we usually end up regretting it in the morning."

"That's pre-Dr. Ive to you." Kelly pointed at her with the miniature parasol that had been perched in her large, salt-rimmed glass. "And we never have regrets. It's a rule."

Oh yeah. She could tell. She was going to regret this.

How could a person whisper and yell at the same time? Gabriel sat up in the guest bedroom he'd been borrowing from Bethany and BD for the past week, and listened as the voices filtered in through his open window.

"Tell the driver to wait for us, Ive."

"Be quiet, Kelly. Do you want the neighbors to call the magical voodoo police?"

A burst of rich laughter jerked him to his feet. He hadn't recognized the voices, but he knew that laugh.

Angelique was here?

He kept the light off and walked to the window, glancing down at the driveway below. What in God's name was she up to?

A taxi idled at the curb while three women weaved giddily up the walk. Angelique was in the middle, shaking her head as the other two dragged her closer to the house.

"They're asleep. The lights are out. You won't see anything anyway."

One of the other women tugged on her arm. "You enjoyed the lap dance, didn't you? That was for you. This hunt is for us."

Gabriel's lips quirked. They were drunk. He'd been in that state often enough to recognize the signs. It also sounded like they'd been having a wild night. And if he was reading the situation correctly, Angelique's friends weren't quite ready for it to be over.

He grabbed a pair of well-worn jeans lying on the end of the bed, quickly sliding into them as he headed down the stairs before the women woke the rest of the house.

He didn't want to admit he was in a rush to see her.

He'd been here a week now, lying low until his cuts and bruises faded, fantasizing about Angelique, and learning what he could from BD.

The man was a welcoming host, and a great talker, but getting him to say anything about the things he'd seen as a Loa was a herculean task that Gabriel had yet to manage.

All BD would say was that his memory wasn't what it used to be. Or that the Loa were called the Mysteries for a reason. He did think more would come to him, especially if Gabriel could tell him, specifically, what he was looking for. Then he'd smile, letting Gabriel know without words that it would take information to get any in return.

Gabriel wasn't sure he could tell him anything if he wanted to. Not anything he would believe, anyway. He hardly remembered what had happened himself. His one witness, Emmanuel, had been noticeably absent the last few days, so there was no one around to fill in the blanks.

Bethany had been harder to avoid. That woman was brilliant and abnormally tenacious. Despite his silence on the subject, and her obvious curiosity, she'd kept his family at bay and treated him as a welcome guest. It was easy to see why his sister was so fond of her.

How she would react to this strange, late-night intrusion wasn't clear. Gabriel, however, couldn't be more fascinated.

He opened up the side door and leaned against the frame, waiting to be noticed.

Angelique had grabbed the collar of the taller girl's blouse, unintentionally causing her to choke. "Kelly, please. I told you in confidence. I'll get you an autographed picture, I promise. I'll buy you those matching tutus we passed in the shop. Anything. Ive, tell her to be reasonable."

The woman named Kelly turned, laughing even as she pried Angelique's fingers off her shirt. "Relax, Ang. We aren't going to kidnap him or anything. And stop tempting me with tutus. Think about how brilliant this is—we could charge people. Why not? They have haunted tours and vampire tours . . . We could do *this*."

He'd been enjoying the show, but he couldn't resist interjecting a note of reason. He didn't think Bethany or BD would appreciate becoming a stop on the tourist route. "By *this*, do you mean trespass on private property in the middle of the night and look in other people's windows?"

Three surprised shrieks had him wincing, coming closer, and raising his hands apologetically. "I'm sorry. I didn't mean to scare you."

The smaller one, Ive, recovered first. "Are you him? Angelique, what were you talking about? He's *not* too pretty at all. More the rough and dangerous type. He looks like he just came out on the winning end of a boxing match . . . or a highly physical session in the bedroom. *Bebe*, he's absolutely perfect."

"You forgot to mention he's practically naked, Ive. Jackpot!"

He caught Angelique's horrified gaze and started to laugh. He wasn't sure how she did it, but she continuously took him by surprise. After their last encounter, he hadn't thought anything could embarrass the bold, fearless beauty. Her blush was disarming. Enchanting. And funny as hell.

She covered her face with her hands and peered through her fingers. "Gabriel? What are you doing here?"

He crossed his arms. "Me? I'm an invited guest. What are you doing here? And who do you have with you?"

"Wait—this isn't Bone Daddy? *This* is Gabriel? *The* Gabriel?"

He could feel his smile growing. He couldn't help it. "*The* Gabriel? Well, I'm the only one I know. Why? Has she been talking about me?"

"Has she been talking about yo—"

He watched as Ive whipped Kelly around and stopped her

midsentence. "Kel? Remember those discussions we've had about over-sharing?"

"Of course I do."

The other woman stared at her in meaningful silence until Kelly grasped her meaning. "Oh. Oh, damn." She turned to Angelique. "I'm sorry. I'm horrible. I shouldn't do shots. Get me away from the umbrella drinks and all I do is talk and talk and talk. Do you think that was why the stripper asked if I wanted to be gagged? I thought he was just being kinky."

Gabriel snorted, deciding it was time to get the conversation back on track. "The taxi driver is looking impatient, and he's probably charging you a fortune." He smirked. "He might even be calling the voodoo police. If you'd like, I could give you three a ride home."

Of course, he'd have to swipe Bethany's keys, but he'd deal with the fallout later. He just wanted to spend more time with Angelique, though he didn't want to think about why right now.

"No, no. We have to go. Come on, girls. I think we've made enough regrets for the night. For the year." Angelique swayed on her feet as she spoke, and he came closer, ready to catch her.

Her friends weren't faring much better. And they had horrible poker faces. The blonde nudged the woman beside her. "Look, we have to take the taxi back to the hotel. We're exhausted. But Angelique doesn't have a way home. You could take her, Gabriel. Just you two. Together. Alone in her apartment. Without us."

Did one of them just wink at him?

Angelique groaned and dropped her chin to her chest, her long curls spilling over her shoulders and hiding her face. "When the world stops spinning I am going to get you both back, you know."

They walked down the drive, leaving Angelique behind, and giggling like a pair of teenagers. "We know," one of them sing-songed. "But it will be worth it. We'll call you tomorrow."

Gabriel watched the taxi drive away, hoping the driver knew where he was going, because he was close to certain neither of the women would.

After a few minutes of silence he started to worry she had fallen asleep standing up. "Angelique?"

"I was hoping you were a tequila-induced hallucination," she muttered.

He thought about Emmanuel. "I've been there before. Unfortunately for you, I'm real."

She sighed. "I figured." Her hands came up to push her hair back, revealing a rueful expression. "My old roommates. They're harmless. Usually. I should never have told them about BD."

"Why did you?"

She huffed. "We tell each other everything. It's a girlfriend rule."

He narrowed his gaze. "Everything? Is that why I'm *the* Gabriel?"

Angelique lifted her chin, one high-pitched hiccup the only sign that she was impaired. "Yes, I'll admit to that. You are *the* Gabriel. But you don't know if you're *the* Gabriel, my mysteriously sexy dream lover, or *the* Gabriel, my friend's irritating brother who is absolutely no fun at dinner parties."

He just stared at her, and after a minute or two, she began to smile. A minute more and a chuckle escaped from between her lips. She held out her arms helplessly. "There's no way to get out of this with dignity. And I'm too tipsy to try. I just hope we didn't wake Bethany up. She's been really nice to me."

He reached out and took her hand, drawing her closer to the door. "Me, too. But we would have known by now. Trust me. Come inside. I'll get dressed; then I can drive you home."

She didn't argue, and he was grateful. Just her hand in his, and he wasn't sure he would be able to let her go. The same intensity. The same need as before.

He opened the door and stepped aside to let her walk in ahead of him. It was an old-school habit with benefits. He closed his eyes as that lush body slid against him, her soft, sweet-smelling hair brushed over his bare chest.

She walked through the darkened kitchen to the small break-fast table. The outside light came through the window and it seemed to be shining on her.

Poetry again. He was in sorry shape. It was obvious his resistance when it came to Angelique Rousseau was nonexistent. Hadn't he told himself a thousand times this week to stay away from her? Now she was here, she needed a ride home, and all he could think about was bending her over that table and lifting her skirt to reveal the biteable ass beneath. She'd make those sounds he loved as he spread her legs. And then he'd take her. The way he had every night in his mind.

"I've been having the craziest dreams about you lately."

Angelique's voice was hushed in the darkness, but it jolted him out of his fantasy. He moved closer. "What was I doing?"

She turned around to face him, her hand going up to her temple as she swayed. "Oops, I think I turned too fast."

Hell, he'd forgotten. "You've been drinking."

She huffed out a laugh. "Without a doubt."

He took a step closer. "I'm supposed to be a gentleman."

Her warm brown eyes were sparkling. "Even in my current condition I could argue that point."

One last step and he was right in front of her. She tilted her head back to look up at him. "Don't you want to hear about my dreams?"

He clenched his fists, nails biting into his palms as he tried to restrain himself from touching her. "That might not be a good idea."

"There you go again. Throwing down a challenge I won't be able to resist." Angelique reached out to touch his chest and he clenched his jaw.

"You've been hurt." Her soft hand skimmed along his rib cage. Tracing the fading but still-colorful bruises there.

"You mentioned my bad habits before, remember? I accidentally ran into a fist or two the other night." He remembered the shadows. Yet another reason he should resist her.

She nodded, a wrinkle of worry forming between her arched brows. "You should replace a few of your habits with something less dangerous." She bit her lip, the backs of her fingers swirling around his hard nipples. "Ive was right. You are absolutely perfect."

Gabriel groaned, wondering why he'd ever thought he stood a chance against her. Against this. "You're the dangerous one. Do you know that?"

He didn't wait for her answer. He gripped her hips and lifted her onto the table, taking her mouth with a ferocity that should have shocked him. Any finesse he had was gone, but she didn't seem to mind.

If anything, she matched his wildness. Demanding just as much. Needing just as much. Her nails scratched his back as she pulled him closer and he growled. Loving the sensation.

Then she was reaching for his hand and placing it underneath her skirt, between her thighs. He hissed at the feel of her damp, cotton panties beneath his fingertips. She covered his fingers with her own and pressed down against her clit, massaging herself in firm, swift circles, showing him how she wanted to be touched. This was what he needed. Not the fantasy. Not the dream of her. He wanted raw sex and real passion.

Energy surged through him. Power. Touching her did this to him. But he had to have more. He had to have everything.

His fingers slipped beneath the elastic band and cotton fabric to touch her and he moaned as her arousal soaked his skin.

He lifted his mouth and she sighed. "Gabriel, you're making me so dizzy. How are you doing that?"

His free hand stilled on the zipper of his pants as her words splashed over him like an icy wave. He wanted to believe it was him, his kiss that made her dizzy, but he knew that wasn't entirely true. He could taste the tequila mixed with Angelique's unique flavor on his tongue. He knew she wasn't in complete control.

A second ago it didn't matter. He wanted her too much. So much he hadn't thought about where they were or what he was doing. A vein on his temple throbbed. He hadn't even thought about condoms.

His body didn't care. His cock was still trying to punch a hole through his jeans and his hand was still between her legs, craving the contact.

But satisfying this craving wouldn't happen unless he was the only thing affecting her senses.

Maybe he was a fucking gentleman after all.

He took his hand from beneath her skirt. Slipping his arm beneath her legs and his other around her back, he cradled her in his arms.

Angelique smiled up at him, then leaned her head on his shoulder. "You're carrying me to bed? I never pictured you as a romantic."

"Neither did I." His thoughts were grim. "You need to sleep, Angelique. And I need a cold shower. Maybe an ice bath."

"Sleep?" She yawned. "You're not taking me up there to sleep, are you?"

He walked up the stairs slowly, reveling in the weight of her in his arms. Her scent. She cuddled closer, humming a little under her breath, and his lips twitched.

"Quit wriggling or I might change my mind."

She laughed softly, and then her breathing began to change. Slow and deep. She'd fallen asleep. Too bad. Parts of him had really been hoping she'd change his mind.

He got to his bedroom door and angled his body to carry her inside without disturbing her.

"Sleepwalking?"

Gabriel tightened his grip on Angelique and looked up to see BD standing in the shadows. "Not quite."

His host smiled, studying the bundle in Gabriel's arms. "She is special, isn't she? And stronger than her brother gives her credit for. I've always known that."

Gabriel shook his head. "You think you can do anything when you're young."

"She's not that young." BD laughed. "But if that makes your stay on the couch more comfortable tonight, keep thinking it." He pointed toward his bedroom down the hall and lowered his voice. "Bethany's orders."

The two men shared a look of masculine understanding and Gabriel nodded. "That was the plan."

BD turned away and Gabriel could have sworn he heard the man mutter, "What a shame."

His thoughts exactly.

CHAPTER 6

"HERE, ALLEGRA BROUGHT YOU SOMETHING FROM CAFÉ Bwe."

Angelique smiled gratefully at Bethany, accepting the steaming coffee. "My brother may be a pain, but he makes a damn fine cup of go juice. This might just save my life."

The jury was still out on whether or not it was worth saving. How had she let her friends talk her into drinking that much?

Bethany had woken her up this morning with a knowing grin and no mercy. Despite her hangover, Angelique had allowed herself to be pushed into the shower and dragged to Mambo Toussaint's voodoo shop.

After what she did last night, she deserved a little suffering.

She glanced up at Bethany and blushed, hurriedly taking a sip of hot liquid and promptly scalding her tongue. Lovely.

Bethany made a *tsk*ing sound and patted her on the shoulder. "Quit beating yourself up. As far as I'm concerned, nothing happened. I picked you up this morning so we could help the Mambo with some spring cleaning." She paused, looking over her shoulder at the others, before lowering her voice. "We seem to be making a habit of this. Me covering for you. Not that I'm complaining. Just . . . be careful." She moved as if to step away, then added, "But if your friends try to ogle my husband through our windows again, I can't be held responsible for my actions."

Angelique wondered if a person could melt into the floor from embarrassment. Ive and Kelly were a fearless duo at the best of times, but even she hadn't thought they would actually go through with it.

Gabriel had seen her like that. Intoxicated and behaving like a teenager with a crush. He'd touched her. She supposed she should be grateful that he'd been the one to stop this time, before they were interrupted. A drunken romp on someone else's kitchen table was not what she wanted to be regretting this morning.

Liar.

She looked around the back room of Mambo Toussaint's voodoo shop, which was closed for the day. The usually busy store was still and quiet. The shelves filled with oils and herbs, the racks of books about the occult, stood unfondled while

Mambo Toussaint, Ben's mother, Elise Adair, and Bethany chattered over unopened boxes.

The Mamas. Seeing them together, so different and yet so perfectly in sync after a lifetime of friendship, always made her smile. One a colorfully attired voodoo priestess and the mother of Michelle and Gabriel, the other a blonde, always perfectly groomed and elegantly dressed socialite, married to a successful Louisiana businessman. And now they had adopted Angelique's mother, Theresa, folding her into their lives and hearts as though she'd always been there.

But Angelique was glad her mother and sister-in-law weren't around. Or Michelle. She didn't think she could look them in the eye just yet after her childish display.

At least Bethany forgave her. Or this particular chore was putting it out of her mind. She watched the rapture on her new ally's face as Bethany opened a box of old, dusty books.

"You have the best job in the universe, Mama Toussaint." Bethany gasped as she lifted one thick, frayed tome. "People just give you these?"

Angelique stood and wandered toward them curiously as the Mambo nodded in answer. "I've purchased a thing or two at different estate sales, but for the most part yes. Old family members who have no one left to pass their knowledge to, hougans and practitioners who wish to ensure their legacy lives on until it can be passed to the next generation—they send their collections to me."

The Mambo opened another box and pulled out a long

strand of blown-glass beads and bone. "Some things are sold, many are given away to those truly interested . . . but some objects are too powerful and are entrusted to me to keep safe for as long as I can. Until another keeper comes along."

Elise moved to the other side of the Mambo and placed a warm hand on her shoulder. "Very subtle, Annemarie."

The Mambo glared at her before turning her obsidian gaze back to Bethany.

Bethany started. "Me? Are you talking about me?"

Did she sound hopeful? It sounded like a major homework to Angelique, but then, she'd never met anyone so interested in books and history as Bethany was. Even with a sensual powerhouse of a husband to distract her, she still found time for her other great obsession.

The Mambo's expression was serene. "I'm not planning on going anywhere just yet, but I would like you to catalogue some of the older, personal journals for me. I know you don't practice the faith, but you are connected to it all the same. Who else do you know who's been on the other side of the Gate of Guinee and back? Who, other than you, has been granted an audience with Papa Legba *and* brought home a Loa of her very own?"

Angelique stepped closer. She knew the stories about the gate. Every New Orleans teen who'd snuck out of the house to go to a party, who had to walk past one of the cemeteries late at night, knew *not* to look for it. "Wait—that's real? Is that how BD became human? Bethany found it?"

The three women turned toward her as if just remembering

she was there. Elise nodded at the same time Bethany shook her head.

"I wouldn't have known about it if not for them." She gestured toward the Mamas. "And Emmanuel."

"Emmanuel?"

Elise smiled, clearly delighted. "She hasn't heard the whole story yet, has she? How about we have our coffee and tell her before we work?" She scrunched her nose at Annemarie. "And I'm not just saying that because I don't like getting dirty. Everything happens for a reason, yes? Angelique is one of the family now; she deserves to hear the highlights. Should we start with Bone Daddy waking up naked in the cemetery? I love that part."

Angelique closed her mouth, which had dropped open at Elise's very visual teaser. "Now you have to tell me."

Sipping the rapidly cooling liquid, she listened, utterly enthralled as Bethany told her the whole story of how she and Bone Daddy met and fell in love, of their tragic past life together and the Loa's intervention, as well as the young ghost Emmanuel's sweetness and sacrifice.

She'd known the basics, information garnered from eavesdropping and Allegra's writing, but nothing this detailed. "That is the most romantic story I've ever heard."

But a little sad. Angelique found herself feeling sorry for the boy who'd died so young, who'd spent so many years trying to share the truth about what happened to his sister and her lover. And then, when he'd found them at last, a family and people who could see him, he had to leave them again.

"Poor Emmanuel."

She hadn't realized she'd spoken out loud until Bethany took her hand gratefully. "Thank you for that. He deserves to be remembered. And I do miss him, but he wanted to go. I have to believe he's happy. That he is where he is destined to be. And with what I know now about life . . . I believe, in one way or another, we'll see each other again."

Then her deep blue eyes narrowed, and she tilted her head. "In fact, I could have sworn I heard him the other day. Or someone who sounded a lot like him. Like I'd imagined he would sound if he'd grown up."

The older women leaned closer. "You did? Was that how you knew about my . . ." Mambo Toussaint took a calming breath. "About the fight?"

Bethany nodded. "Yes, but I know it wasn't him. It couldn't be. Still . . . who? And why me? Why didn't whoever it was go to Michelle or one of you?"

Angelique was lost. The fight? She remembered the fading bruises on Gabriel's body. They must be talking about him— and a disembodied voice that had led help to him . . .

She looked at the Mambo. "It might be the same voice that talks to him."

Now all eyes were focused on her, and, standing behind the other women, Bethany was shaking her head in warning.

Elise pushed a lock of shiny blonde hair behind one ear. "A voice talks to him? How could you know that, dear?"

Uh-oh. Maybe she shouldn't have said anything. "I— Um, well. I was out in Ben and Michelle's backyard look— I mean getting some air." She covered her racing heart with her hand, feeling the same way she had when she'd told her mother that Leroy Cavuti had given her a hickey. "I heard Gabriel yelling at someone, but when he saw me he said he was just talking to himself."

The Mambo swayed and Elise wrapped an arm around her, leading her to the nearest chair.

Angelique didn't need any special abilities to know what they were all thinking. That it was the *djab*. That the thing they couldn't place, the feeling they all had around him since he'd returned was what they'd most feared. But she knew it wasn't true. She wasn't sure how she knew; she just did.

She knelt beside the Mambo with an earnest expression. "It told Bethany how to help him, right? And when I heard him, he sounded like he was arguing with a really irritating pest, not anything evil." She thought about the conversation she'd had with BD and Bethany, grasping for another explanation. "For all we know, it could be those Marassa Twins. Or a guardian angel."

Gabriel wasn't evil. Rude, insensitive, and aggravatingly arrogant, certainly, but not evil. Angelique fiddled with her cross again, praying her instincts were right. That the man she was lusting after, feeling protective of, wasn't irredeemable. That she wasn't as wrong about him as her mother had been about her father.

"BD would agree with her."

Angelique glanced up over her shoulder at Bethany, who was biting her lip. Was she holding something back, or concerned that Angelique had said too much?

Mambo Toussaint spoke in a soft, gentle voice. "Elise is right. You are here for a reason. A very special spirit to be so kind. Theresa is wise to be proud of you, though I think, just like any mother would, she still sees you as the baby she held in her arms. But you're a woman, aren't you? Elise, I think we are getting old."

Elise Adair made a dismissive sound. "Impossible. I'm sure I would've noticed something like that." She, too, looked down at Angelique, reaching out to place a hand on her arm.

Angelique recognized her expression. Her son, Ben, had worn it each time he'd searched her mind, looking for the truth. Oh damn, how could she have let herself forget?

She tried to push away the memories of her and Gabriel together, but from the startled look on Elise's face, she knew she hadn't succeeded. Angelique blushed.

"She is definitely grown-up now," Elise murmured. "But I think she's right—nothing negative has control of him. Still, there *is* something going on with Gabriel. Something he hasn't seen fit to tell his family."

Angelique could relate. Hadn't she been avoiding her own family? Not only keeping her growing feelings for Gabriel a secret, but also not telling them about turning down the job one of her professors had offered her with the Atchafalaya National Wildlife Refuge?

She'd been drawn home again, at a crossroads in her life, trying to decide what she really wanted for her future. Dragged back here as if by an unseen hand. She didn't know why. She'd thought she wanted the job. She'd worked for it.

Until recently, she'd been planning on making a permanent home in Baton Rouge, close to her friends and the life she'd built for herself over the past few years. Where she wasn't the innocent who needed to be protected from all the family skeletons. From life. But something had been missing. She'd come back to New Orleans to discover what it was. Though since she'd returned, questions about her future had taken a backseat to her preoccupation with Gabriel.

"Maybe you will find your answers soon, little angel."

Shit. Elise was still touching her. Angelique stood up quickly, distancing herself from the petite empath. She wondered how Michelle did it, marrying into a family who knew every random thought in your head. It was disconcerting.

Mambo Toussaint rescued her from having to respond. "Leave the poor girl alone, Elise. She's come here to work, she's relieved an old mama's mind, and she doesn't need us giving her the mental third degree." She placed her hands on her thighs and leaned forward until she was standing again. She smiled at Angelique. "It's enough for now to know he's safe from that evil. My son came home. And he'll come to me with his burden in his own time."

Elise seemed dubious, but nodded in agreement. "Let's start unpacking these boxes, then. The longer we wait, the dustier they get."

Mambo Toussaint chortled. "Ain't that the plain truth? Angelique, I think there's a box of protection fetishes and jewelry around here somewhere. If you find something good, maybe you can keep it as payment for helping us go through everything. Just let me see it first. Bethany, I put those journals around here somewhere . . ."

She turned away and Angelique shared a look of relief with Bethany, heading to the box farthest away from Elise Adair. She was grateful that Ben's mother hadn't mentioned her encounters with Gabriel to the Mambo, but she wanted to keep her thoughts to herself, thank you very much. The smartest move, in her opinion, since so many of them these days were X-rated.

The hours passed swiftly as the foursome dug into the pile of other people's memories. Angelique hadn't realized it would be this engrossing. That the figurines made of seashells or the rings made of twine would make her feel like an explorer discovering buried treasure.

Mixed in with the trinkets were old photographs of women and men from a time when New Orleans was younger, the clapboards brighter, and life filled with more promise and vitality.

Back then there was no graffiti, no areas of town cordoned off by orange tape, no bad memories that everyone wanted to forget. She knew Louisiana had never been an easy place for people to live. They'd carved their cities out of the bayou and swamp, daring the elements to take away what they'd created. Though nature had tried on many occasions, the people always came back, more defiant than ever.

But Hurricane Katrina had been different. New Orleans hadn't bounced back with its usual resilience. Sure, the main tourist attractions were back in business, people were still drinking to excess, riding in horse-drawn carriages and having beignets at Café Dumond. But beneath the glitter of the beads and celebrations, the melody of the city had changed.

Each time she'd come home on vacation from school, Angelique had looked for it, what she remembered from her childhood. It hadn't gone away completely; people were building houses and repairing what had been lost. Others, like her, had gone to school with the intention of fixing what had been broken. But she knew in her heart it would never be completely the same.

She lifted the yellowed picture in her hand, staring at the proud, smiling figure with a white kerchief covering her curls. New Orleans would never again be the place *this* woman had known.

A tinny, musical sound drew her gaze to the corner of the room. A small bookshelf filled with shoe boxes. She heard it again and Angelique glanced at the others, wondering if they heard it, too. No one glanced up from their work. Strange.

Angelique set down the picture and got to her feet, walking until she was standing right in front of the bookshelf. The shoe box directly in her line of vision moved. Her brows furrowed in disbelief.

Maybe she needed more coffee.

She turned to go back to her sorting when something hit her right between her shoulder blades. Angelique looked down on the floor. "What the—?" A box lid was lying there as if it had tossed itself at her.

She grumbled under her breath about the dangers of voo-doo shops, bending to pick it up and cover the box once more.

"Oh, how pretty."

Right on top, spread out as though waiting to be admired, was an antique locket. A beautiful piece of jewelry with delicate, silver filigreed leaves and vines, leading to a single ruby-red gem. A rose. Inside the frame of vines the locket looked as though it had once had an engraving, but it had been worn away so much Angelique knew that more than time was involved.

She reached for it, feeling the weight in her palm. It was warm. She tried to open it but the latch was sealed. It appeared that the silver there had melted, and there were still traces of wax along the seams.

Someone hadn't wanted this to be opened.

Still, it was stunning. Holding it in her hands made her cheeks flush.

"You okay?" Bethany showed up beside her, her arms full of books.

"I'm fine. You are definitely in your element."

Bethany didn't bother to hide her grin. "Absolutely. This is fascinating." She lowered her voice. "I was just asking. Celestin isn't very comfortable with this kind of thing because of your—"

"Father, I know." Angelique stopped her, knowing where she was going. "I'm the youngest. I mean, my memories of the old man aren't good, but I have a lot less of them. And I didn't have to suffer the consequences of my father's deal."

The deal he'd made with Bone Daddy. The deal that offered

the bodies of his children in return for the adoration of the one woman in town who wouldn't sleep with him.

Bone Daddy. BD. Angelique shook her head. "We are a very unlikely group, aren't we?"

Bethany shrugged. "I don't know. On the outside maybe that's true. But something brought us together, magic or hoo-doo, whatever you want to call it. And love kept us close. Personally, I like us. And I've never been fond of people as a rule." She hugged the journals to her chest. "Books, on the other hand . . ."

The two women laughed just as Angelique showed Bethany her prize. "I just found this. The lid . . . fell off and there it was. Do you think the Mambo will let me have it?"

Beth studied it and frowned. "You should ask, just to make sure, but she did say you could pick something you wanted."

"Why do you think they sealed it like this?" Angelique's voice was hushed. She felt so strange. Breathless. And she couldn't take her gaze away from the locket.

"I'm not sure." Bethany sounded thoughtful. "From what I've read, it's done to keep the essence of something close. Locked inside. Love or protection, things like that. Maybe a woman was trying to keep her lover from roaming."

Angelique grimaced. She couldn't imagine allowing herself to get that desperate. If she couldn't get Gabriel on her own, no magical spell would do. She'd learned that much from her father's mistakes.

Still, she wanted this necklace. If it was a fetish used to bind a lover, then maybe it would serve as a reminder for her not to be so blinded by lust that she lost her bearings.

A reminder she might need if she spent too much more time around Gabriel. It was an idea that didn't scare her the way it should have.

Not a good sign.

CHAPTER 7

"WHEN ARE YOU GOING TO TELL US WHAT'S GOING ON with you?"

Gabriel froze in the act of putting on a clean shirt. "Bethany. I didn't hear you come in."

At least she'd waited until he'd gotten out of the shower. She would have gotten an eyeful of more than just his naked behind, and he would have been too busy trying to ease the relentless, bottomless ache in his cock to notice her arrival.

Just thinking about his most recent fantasy involving Angelique Rousseau made his erection stir again. Jesus. He needed to go out and get laid. Get this out of his system. Preferably with someone he didn't know.

"Well?"

Bethany crossed her arms, tapping her toe on the wood floor, making him feel like a child about to be reprimanded.

Gabriel sat down on the bed, buttoning his shirt. "I really appreciate you letting me stay here. It's been . . . helpful."

He'd been surprised to find the same kind of protection in this house as he had at his mother's. No shadows. He shouldn't have been. BD did know all the tricks of the trade, after all. And he'd felt good here, but he knew it wouldn't last. He still didn't know what he was or why. And he still didn't feel like he could tell them about Emmanuel.

"I should go."

Bethany tilted her head, as though studying a strangely colored bug. "Probably. But for some reason I don't want you to. Maybe it has something to do with the voice I heard the night we found you, but I feel responsible for you. Besides, unless you're willing to tell your mother what you won't tell me, I think you'll do less damage under my roof."

Gabriel flinched. She sounded like Emmanuel. Had he done damage? Had his silence caused his mother pain? His sister? God, he was an ass. "So I can stay?"

She was silent for so long he began to mentally consider hotel options; then she shrugged one shoulder. "You can't hide forever—Michelle would kill me if I let you—but yes, you can stay. You have to earn your keep, though."

Bethany crooked her finger at him before turning to walk down the hall. Intrigued, Gabriel followed. They walked down the stairs in silence until they reached the black-and-white marble table in the foyer. Bethany picked up a large, sealed envelope and handed it to him.

"Angelique forgot this at your mother's shop today. I have too much to do but I really need her to get this tonight. It's important."

A blow to the head wouldn't have shocked him more. Despite his body's immediate response, he shook his head. "You know that isn't a good idea."

"What isn't a good idea, Blue Eyes?"

BD appeared from the living room and Gabriel swore under his breath. He'd been looking for the bastard all morning, determined to get some answers, but he'd been nowhere to be found.

Bethany lifted her cheek for her husbands gentle kiss, leaning back against him affectionately. "I asked him to make a simple delivery, but Gabriel is afraid he won't be able to resist Rousseau's little sister."

BD pursed his lips thoughtfully, Gabriel watching as his hands caressed Bethany's hips, pulling her closer against him. "He has a point, *cher*. You saw what happened at the dinner party. And the other night in our driveway."

"Thanks for the vote of confidence." He *could* resist her, damn it. He just had a hard time remembering that when he was close enough to smell her. To see those luscious breasts begging for his touch.

He watched the couple in front of him, wondering what kind of game they were playing. If they were aiming to make a match, they were going to be in for a major disappointment. They were also going to bring down the wrath of Rousseau, one of BD's closest friends.

A fact that might save him from this delivery. "I think Celestin would rather I stay far away from his little sister. Especially since I'm so mysterious and scary."

"Something you could fix whenever you wanted." Bethany rolled her eyes. "But regardless, I'm asking you to do it as a favor to me."

BD waggled his eyebrows. "Aren't you getting the hint? My blushing bride wants to be alone with me. I was thinking sex on the kitchen table, maybe a little role-playing where I am the plumber and she is a naked woman in my clutches."

Bethany looked over her shoulder at her husband, her lips quirking in helpless amusement. "A plumber is not the first fantasy I would pick."

BD pouted playfully. "But you said it turned you on when I fixed the garbage disposal."

Gabriel grabbed the envelope. "On that disturbing note." He opened the door and took a deep, fortifying breath. He could do this. Bethany and BD hadn't asked him for anything. Plus, they'd saved his life. He could hand one package over to the saucy, aggravating Angelique without attacking her as soon as she opened the door.

He hoped.

Gabriel knew within minutes of hopping into his rental car that Emmanuel was with him. "Where have you been?"

"Other than giving you some privacy for your wackathon?"

Emmanuel mocked. "I've been around. You know, there are more interesting things going on this city than watching you mope."

Gabriel's hands clenched on the steering wheel. "More interesting than whatever's happening to me? More interesting than ghosts and Loas and blackouts where I turn into the ninja from Hell? This should be good."

Emmanuel, who was reclining in the backseat of the Mercedes, sighed. "As a matter of fact, yes. You know, when I was here before, all I could see was my tiny little corner of the world. The house where I grew up. You and Michelle and the family who purchased the house from mine. I had no idea that more than that existed. No one told me."

"If you're trying to scare me, you'll have to do better than that. Who never told you what?"

Emmanuel suddenly appeared in the seat beside him, his intensely blue eyes sparkling. "Others. Not Loa. Not like me, either. At least, not that I've met yet." He studied Gabriel, then shook his head, smiling. "Let's just say Angelique's professor may have something to his teachings, after all."

Gabriel sneered. "You seen a Loup Garou recently, Manny? Great. Maybe you should go pop in on *him* when he least expects it. Drive someone else crazy for a change."

"There's more, but I can see you're not interested. That stick up your ass wouldn't have anything to do with seeing Angelique again, would it? Or have you finally come to your senses? Are you on your way to tell the Mambo what you can do?"

"BD doesn't even know; I don't even know; why should my mother? You're like a damn broken record." Gabriel's shoulders were so tense they were practically pressing against his ears. "Why don't you tell me?"

Emmanuel huffed out a frustrated breath. "Why don't *you* tell *me*? Have you even tried to figure it out for yourself? What do you think happened the other night?"

He'd seen the darkness, and then it had seen him. It came into him and he'd blacked out, apparently kicking the shit out of the street toughs who had him sorely outnumbered. "It wasn't possession."

"Not in the sense you know it. But I already told you that."

"It was clinging to those men."

Emmanuel nodded. "It looks for their own. Seeks out certain energies, certain people."

"Now we're back to square one. I draw the darkness; therefore I'm a dick for bringing that wonderful gift home to my family. Thanks for clearing that up."

Emmanuel frowned. "Why are we going to see the girl, anyway?"

Was he trying to change the subject? Gabriel sneered. "Some disembodied voice spoke to Bethany, telling her where I was the other night. She was upset that I wouldn't tell her what I knew about that." He sent Emmanuel a meaningful glance. "So I'm running errands, trying to get back into her good graces."

"Oh. That." Emmanuel sucked his bottom lip into his mouth, lowering his head, his dark hair swooping over his face to hide his expression. "She was the closest."

"Whatever you want to tell yourself, Manny. But for someone who keeps telling me I need to talk to my mama, you seem to have a few familial communication issues of your own."

He pulled up to park along the curb in front of the old apartment building Angelique was staying in and turned off the car.

Emmanuel reached for his arm before he could open the door. "Gabe, I have a bad feeling. I don't think you should go up there."

Gabriel laughed, but the sound was grim. "You and me both, buddy. That girl is more dangerous than she looks." And he hadn't been able to get her out of his mind. It didn't help that his pillow still smelled of her. That he knew she'd showered in his bathroom, slept in his bed last night.

He walked around the front of his car to find Emmanuel already standing in front of the door. "Seriously, I don't think it's a good idea. Angelique isn't why you're here. She's not part of the plan."

Gabriel raised a suspicious brow. "Angelique, huh? If I didn't know any better, I'd think you were worried about her, not me. Is it because of what I am? Because of this mysterious plan you won't tell me anything about? Or maybe you can't forget the way she looked, spread out on the grass, begging for me to fuck her. Does Manny have a little crush?"

Gabriel pushed past Emmanuel and opened the door that would lead him to the stairs up to her apartment.

"You'll hurt her."

He froze, refusing to look into judgmental blue eyes. A

judgment he didn't disagree with. The closer he got to her door, the more thoroughly he sealed his fate. This time he wouldn't push Angelique away. He wouldn't leave until he knew what it was like to be inside her. Regardless of the consequences.

"Then stop me, Manny. Because I don't think I can stop myself."

The silence turned Gabriel around on the staircase. Emmanuel was gone. He was alone, his guardian angel nowhere in sight. His only hope now rested with Angelique.

Heaven help them both.

ANGELIQUE SAT ON THE WORN, COMFORTABLE COUCH IN her childhood apartment, lost in thought as the sun began to set outside. Maybe she shouldn't have turned down Ive and Kelly, who'd called her, worried, apologetic, and wanting to come over.

She'd told them she wanted to be alone, though she knew it wasn't true. She wanted to find Gabriel and demand he tell her what he was, why he was here, and what he had done to her.

This wasn't her. She'd never felt this out of control, this crazed. And all because of one man. Gabriel.

But she couldn't blame him for her actions today. She wasn't sure why she'd done it, pocketed the locket without showing it to Mambo Toussaint.

Even though she'd been told she could take something if she wanted it, a small voice in her head had worried that she wouldn't be allowed to keep it. Barely aware of what she was doing, she'd slipped the locket into the pocket of her jeans while Bethany was busy with the Mamas.

She'd also rushed out before Elise Adair could hug her, ensuring that the older woman wouldn't know.

Her gentle, petite mother would tan her backside for her behavior. And for what? Some old necklace?

Angelique studied the piece of jewelry in question. She'd set it on the coffee table, staring at it as if it were a venomous insect preparing to strike.

She'd take it back tomorrow and hope she hadn't offended Michelle and Gabriel's mother. The last thing she needed was to anger a voodoo priestess.

The red gem on the locket glittered in the flickering light of the candles. Angelique looked around the living room ruefully. If a stranger saw this scene, they might imagine that she was in for a romantic evening. Surrounded by candles, a bottle of wine at her side, in nothing but a white satin chemise.

As if she were waiting for her lover.

A dark thread of self-recrimination wound its way into her thoughts. How many nights had her mother waited, after her children had gone to bed, for the man she loved? How many nights had she spent alone, while he ignored her for one mistress after the next, for one dark deed after another?

Theresa Rousseau had not raised her daughter to be dependent on any man. She'd been determined, as had Celestin, that Angelique would have the strength and tools she needed to make her own way in the world. And until now, Angelique had never doubted her path. Her worth.

She wasn't the kind of person who felt the need to hide what she was thinking. Wasn't the kind of woman who had ever chased after a man who'd refused her, offering herself to him again and again, despite his resistance. And she certainly didn't steal from friends.

She knew she needed to get her head on straight, but her body didn't want to cooperate. It still wanted relief. Satisfaction.

Maybe she should call Ive back and tell her she'd changed her mind. That she didn't want to be alone. She stood up and leaned over to blow out the candle in front of her. No more waiting.

The knock on the door made her jump, startled. She laughed softly at herself, relieved that, as usual, her friends hadn't listened to her. They'd come over anyway.

"I should've known you couldn't stay away. What naughty adventure do you two have planned for tonight? I'm ready for anythi—" She swung open the door and her throat closed.

"Expecting someone?"

She couldn't speak. He was here. Gabriel was at her door. She glanced around his body, over his shoulder. And he was alone. She remembered the conversation she'd had with the Mamas and Bethany and mentally reworded her thoughts. He was alone . . . as far as she knew.

Her fingertips dug into the doorframe as she continued to stare at him, watching as her lack of reaction affected his body.

His shoulders tensed and his jaw tightened. She saw his gaze look past her and into the room. He took in her thin slip, the candles on the mantel behind her, and gritted his teeth. "Didn't mean to interrupt your plans for the evening. I'm just here to deliver something from Bethany."

Bethany? She looked down at the envelope he stretched out in her direction, having a hard time putting a coherent thought together.

She'd seen Bethany just a few hours ago. Why hadn't she given this to her earlier? Then a sudden, jarring worry clenched her heart. What if she knew what Angelique had done? Was it a warning to return the locket? That didn't seem like Bethany's style.

Gabriel sighed roughly and Angelique straightened. "Come on in."

She turned before he could pass the package to her and go, as he obviously wanted to. "My friends threatened to come over and cheer me up. That's who I thought you were."

Gabriel took a few strides into the room, looking pointedly around at the romantic setting. "The women from the other night? I didn't think you would be up for that sort of thing."

She whirled around in time to catch the teasing glint in his moss-green eyes. "You have no idea what I'm up for."

He inhaled sharply, running fingers through his wavy hair with his free hand, offering the envelope with the other. "Take it."

"No."

"No?" Gabriel's gaze narrowed, studying her stubbornly lifted chin, the lips that felt hot and swollen. Needy. "Fine." He set it on the bar that separated the kitchen from the living room. "I should go."

Angelique crossed her arms over her suddenly aching

breasts. She wasn't begging him. Not this time. "You're probably right."

Neither one of them moved. Angelique watched him struggle; she could practically see the battle being waged in his mind. He wanted her; she knew he did. But maybe he'd been right in the first place. She didn't know what she was getting into with Gabriel. She should stay as far away from him as she could.

"Open it first." Gabriel's voice was rough, that rasp she loved seeming to scrape along her spine, making her shiver.

Why? She furrowed her brow and hesitated. She'd have to walk past him to get the envelope, near enough to touch him. To feel his heat. Was he trying to torture her?

He needed to leave before she threw herself at him again. This time there would be no one to find them, no reason to stop. This time he'd have to reject her without any excuses. She wasn't sure she could deal with that tonight.

"Okay, fine." She took a breath and started past him to reach for the long envelope. "You can tell her you've done your duty and— Hey!"

He dragged her up against his body, his fingers wrapping around her biceps, his gaze trapping hers. "Just sex," he muttered. "I don't have anything else to give. No one else knows; no one gets hurt. Just me, fucking you, until we get this out of our systems."

Hadn't she just been lecturing herself on not being led around by this man? Not letting her obsession cost her her pride? No woman in her right mind would say yes to such a crude offer. But Angelique was coming to realize she wasn't in her right mind, and it was all his fault. He was a fraud. Pretending he chose to be isolated. Pretending he didn't need anyone or anything. But she was on to him.

He wanted just sex? Well, so did she. "Just sex." Her voice was more breathless than she'd have liked as she agreed, but his reaction was more than satisfying.

He shuddered against her, moaning against her mouth. "Where?"

Where what? What was he asking her? How did he expect her to think when she was so close to him? "What?"

Gabriel growled. "Fuck it." He whirled her around and lifted her onto the small dining room table in the corner of the apartment. The same table she'd colored on as a child. Where she'd said her prayers before dinner. Done her homework.

God, why did that idea make her so hot?

He spread her legs and stepped between her thighs, his jeans rough against her bare flesh. He lifted his lips from hers to look into her eyes. "No going back, angel. Not this time."

Thank God. Maybe that locket was lucky, after all.

CHAPTER 8

SHE'D GIVEN HIM AN OUT. HE COULD HAVE LEFT, COULD have walked away, unselfishly sparing her from what he was. On a good day he was a spoiled, arrogant jackass. The not-so-good days, which came more often than not lately, he was so much worse.

But he wasn't one of the good guys. Never had been. He left the heroics to Angelique's brother, to the patient Ben Adair.

Gabriel took what he wanted, when he wanted it. And he wanted her. More than he should.

"Wait."

Fuck. Was she pushing him away? He tried to focus on her, tried to restrain himself from falling on her like a wild, hungry animal.

117

She licked her lush lips as if she were savoring his taste. Damn, she was beautiful. He saw her mouth move, but the blood pounding in his ears made it hard for him to hear her. "What?"

"Undress. I want to see you this time. All of you."

He was having a hard time catching his breath, his hands shaking, cock so hard he was worried this might be over before it began, and she wanted a *striptease*?

But it never crossed his mind to deny her. One button flew across the room as he hurriedly complied. He watched the flush darken her cheeks when he slipped off his shirt and felt a rush of adrenaline. She liked what she saw.

So did he. And he wanted to see more. His hands paused on the brass buttons of his jeans. "I need motivation. Show me those perfect breasts, Angelique. Offer them to me."

She shivered, shrugging her shoulders so the straps of her silk, lace-edged gown slid down bare arms. Gabriel loosened the first button, then the second. Her breasts were so deliciously firm, despite their fullness, that they held the fabric up by themselves.

Her hands slid up, cupping her breasts like a lover before her fingers curled around the lace. Taunting him.

"Little tease." His throat was tight and his mouth watered. He kicked off his shoes and finished unbuttoning his fly, but refused to push the denim down until she complied. Or he lost whatever restraint he had left.

She stared at the patch of tight, dark curls he'd revealed,

her breath coming in short, sexy little pants. "Hello, Pot, this is Kettle."

He laughed in surprise. How did she do that? Get him this crazy and make him love it? Surprise him? "I seem to recall you mentioning a spanking. Is that what you're aiming for, baby? Is that what you want?"

Her brown eyes sparked, and he felt his cock jerk in response. She swallowed, pulling down the ivory satin to reveal her flushed golden skin, the dark nipples peaked and, he already knew, delicious.

He reached for her but she leaned back, her palms bracing on the table as she shook her head. The move arched her back, highlighting the edible breasts that remained just out of reach. "A deal's a deal."

"Tease." But he was fighting a smile. He couldn't help it. He stepped out of his jeans and his hands curled into fists at his side . . . waiting.

Her doe eyes were wide as she studied his thick erection. She sat up straight again, moving closer as she reached out her hand to touch it.

Gabriel gripped her wrist. "That's not a good idea right now, angel."

"It's not?" She sounded distracted. Needy.

He growled. "No." He slid his other hand underneath the skirt of her slip, scraping his short nails across her underwear. She was wet. Hot and wet and he couldn't wait anymore.

"Not this time."

Gabriel released her wrist and cupped her jaw, pulling her close for a deep, openmouthed kiss. Thrusting his tongue deep in her mouth, imagining how good it would feel when he got his cock inside her tight heat.

He leaned forward until her back was pressed against the smooth, wooden table, until she was laid out for him like a feast.

He tore his mouth away from hers and reached for her hips, dragging the fabric concealing her sex down her legs before pressing his hips between them once more.

"Oh God."

He silently echoed her cry. Just this. Finally this. His sensitive shaft rubbing against the wet lips of her pussy. So close to what he wanted. What he needed. He pushed the hem of her slip up around her waist so he could see her pink flesh gleaming as his flushed cock searched for entry. Beautiful.

Her hands reached up to grab him—no, *push* him away. She couldn't—not now. Fuck, not now. He grabbed her arms and pushed them over her head, his hips lining up with hers. The head of his cock slipped inside her, his breath hissing out of his lungs. She was so hot she might burn him alive.

"Wait. Damn it, Gabriel, not without protection!"

He jerked back as though she'd slapped him. Son of a bitch, he'd forgotten. Even when he'd been blackout-drunk, taking home someone he'd met five minutes before, he hadn't forgotten.

What the hell was she doing to him?

He released her and forced himself to step back, away from temptation. "Fuck."

She shook her head, damp curls clinging to her temple. "It's okay. I don't want you to stop. Please. Just— Do you have . . . ?"

He almost wished he didn't. How sick was that? Almost wished she'd been too lost to notice. The feel of her on his bare skin wasn't something he would likely forget.

She didn't want him to stop. Good. Because, condom or not, he wasn't sure he could. He fumbled for the wallet in his jeans, slipping out one of the square foil packets and tearing it open with his teeth.

"Thank God." She watched him roll the condom on with eyes glittering with relief and excitement. His cock pulsed in his palms.

He bit into his cheek as he fit the thin sheath over his rigid erection. "Yeah, well, I only have a handful of these with me. We'll either need to make a run in a few hours or . . . get creative."

Her mouth opened.

Gabriel grinned, the awkward moment over. "You're surprised? Don't those little boys you've played doctor with have any stamina, Angelique? Or is it that you think you can't keep up with me?"

He didn't give her a chance to answer. Gabriel gripped her thighs and pulled them wide, giving himself a view of heaven. "I like this. I've kissed you, touched you here, but I like this the best. Knowing I can see everything. Watch you stretch as I fill you."

Angelique moaned and he bent her knees until they touched her breasts. He let go of one of her thighs and pressed her clit between his finger and thumb, squeezing lightly. "I can do anything I want, can't I? Say it."

"Anything."

Her words ripped away any illusion of control he had. Maybe another time he could tease her, play with her, build her passion over and over again before he gave in to his own needs, but not now.

He wasn't sure if he'd ever be able to maintain his control around her. Being near her, touching her, was like a drug. He felt intoxicated. Powerful. Addicted. He needed more.

The twinge of disappointment at the barrier between them didn't compare to how tight she was. The heat he still felt blazing around him as he slowly thrust his cock inside her.

Her legs lifted up to his shoulders, raising her hips a little off the table, and a rumbling growl stuck in his chest. Yes. She wanted him the same way he wanted her.

He fell onto his forearms, his lips hovering above hers. He watched her reaction when he angled his hips for a deeper thrust, impatient to be inside her completely. Her eyes dilated and her neck arched. Perfect.

"Tight, angel. Wrapped around me so tight."

"Gabriel . . . oh, Gabriel."

His smile felt more like a snarl. "That's what I've been waiting to hear. Do you know how many times I imagined you calling out my name as I fucked you? Do you know how crazy you've been making me?" His words had him thrusting deeper. Harder. "Do you know how hard I was, knowing you were sleeping in my bed? That close, and so fucking willing. I came in my hand just imagining slipping in beside you and spreading your legs."

Angelique cried out, her sex clenching around him as a wave of pleasure shook her.

Gabriel gritted his teeth and lifted off her. Still inside her, still thrusting, he turned her onto her side, lifting one of her legs high so he could fill her.

"Oh, that's good, isn't it, baby? Deeper than before?" She nodded, gasping, and he slung his hips powerfully against her in acknowledgment. "When I had breakfast in the kitchen that morning, I imagined this. You laid out for me on the table, taking you just. Like. This."

She was crying now, her fingers curling against the table as if seeking purchase. Trying to gain her bearings. Pushing harder against him.

He didn't want to stop. Wanted to stay inside her. Her orgasm, stronger this time, had him doubting his ability to last. "Yes, Angelique. God, that feels good."

But he needed more. He adjusted her position again, until her beautiful breasts were hidden, but her luscious ass was in view.

He gripped her hips. "Should I tell you what I imagined doing to you here? Other than spanking you, of course."

She looked over her shoulder at him, her lips soft and open, her eyes sparkling with desire. And a dare.

His grip tightened. "Oh, don't worry. You'll get exactly what you want soon enough. But I don't think I can hold back."

Her ass was too sweet. Round and lush, like silk under his

hands. He bent his knees and picked up a faster rhythm, spreading her cheeks with his fingers and growling at what he saw.

God, he wanted to fuck her there. He made a silent promise to himself that he would.

Angelique cried out, the table shaking and creaking with the power of his thrusts. He watched her grip the edges of the table, hanging on for dear life as he rode her.

"Yes, Gabriel. *Harder.*"

Being inside her was better than any fantasy. He felt everything so intensely; his muscles flexing, heart racing, every inch of him feeling alive and on fire for Angelique.

She screamed and he wanted to shout out in victory as she came again, this one so strong her body was shuddering, bruising his cock with the force of it.

A tidal wave of sensation knocked the breath from his lungs, taking him by surprise and sending him crashing, tumbling, into his orgasm.

Angelique.

Gabriel pressed his forehead against her back, waiting for the world to stop spinning and his heart to slow down. Waiting for the usually instantaneous urge to leave.

It didn't come. Sweet Jesus, it didn't come. He really was in trouble.

WHAT WAS HE DOING HERE? HIS JOB WAS TO WATCH OVER Gabriel, help him discover and overcome his unique ability.

Reunite him with his family. Not watch him fuck the brains out of Celestin Rousseau's little sister.

Emmanuel sighed. He'd been around the man too long; he was starting to think like him. Crass. Vulgar. Dark thoughts.

Right now all he could think about was Angelique. Her curving hips, the way her breasts swayed as Gabriel rocked against her.

He'd seen sex before. Admittedly, most of it from a child's perspective. A ghost with no understanding of how to treat the female of the species beyond braid-pulling and slipping toads into skirt pockets.

He was no longer a child in any way. The hellish road he'd taken just to return had robbed him of most of his innocence.

The unaware Angelique was swiftly stealing away the rest. She was distracting him, distracting Gabriel, and he wasn't sure what to do about it.

He'd had a plan, but other than getting Michelle Toussaint's brother back to New Orleans where he belonged, none of it was working out the way he'd thought it would.

He couldn't protect Gabriel forever. Whether the ungrateful ass knew it or not, Emmanuel had been shielding him from the worst of what was out there. Just until he was ready to handle it. He was still in too dark of a place.

But his charge couldn't think of anything but her.

He watched Gabriel lift her up off the dining table, pulling her close in a passionate kiss. She leaned against him weakly, her beautiful body shimmering with heat and light. There was something about her.

Angelique stepped out of his embrace and smiled coyly, weaving, her body a bit unsteady after their exertion. She headed into the kitchen, where the harsh fluorescent overhead light did nothing to take away from the perfection of her. The sensual sway of her movements, the shimmering curls falling down her back.

He'd gone to a museum once. Seen a painting of Venus rising from the ocean. His teacher had covered his eyes and urged him to the next piece of art, but Emmanuel's gaze had returned to it again and again, drawn to the untouchable woman.

Angelique put his Venus to shame. She could be touched. And much to his chagrin, Emmanuel wanted to.

She offered Gabriel some of her water, but he came up to her, took the glass from her hand, and set it on the counter. Then he dropped to his knees.

Her hands shot out to flatten against the jamb of the narrow kitchen doorway as he lifted one of her legs over his shoulder and opened his mouth over her sex.

Emmanuel licked his lips, wondering how she tasted. What she felt like on Gabriel's tongue.

There could be no doubt how it felt to Angelique. It was evident in the ecstasy on her face. He watched her head fall back, showing the curve of her neck, her nipples, taut once more with desire, and her hips gently pulsing against Gabriel's lips.

Emmanuel shifted on his perch on Angelique's wrought-iron balcony, his hand slipping down to his hardening erection.

Watching her, he could imagine that she knew he was there, that she was letting him see this intimate moment. That she wanted him to.

One of her hands came down to curl in Gabriel's hair, tugging him closer. Her moans drifted through the glass and Emmanuel was tempted to move closer. No one would see him unless he wanted them to.

But part of the excitement was the possibility of being seen. He closed his eyes and imagined Angelique watching him open his pants and grip his hot shaft, stroking it to the rhythm of her cries.

She wouldn't say a word. Wouldn't tell Gabriel because she loved having him there, so close, seeing her pleasure.

He increased the pressure on his flesh, a surprised moan escaping his throat. The fantasy Angelique smiled, encouraging him to stroke faster. Like that. *Yes.*

Emmanuel's eyes opened in shock as a feeling as unfamiliar as it was transcendent rocked through his body just as his gaze met Angelique's. Her wide brown eyes studied him as Gabriel kissed his way up her body.

She saw him. Why didn't she look surprised?

He cloaked himself in darkness, watching her searching gaze study the windowpane, maybe wondering if he'd been an illusion.

He shouldn't have done that. She wasn't his; she was Gabriel's. She was also under the protection of his family.

His family. He needed to focus, to remember his end goal, and to succeed in his mission.

It was the only way he could stay.

CHAPTER 9

ANGELIQUE WAS DIZZY, LIGHT-HEADED FROM THE INTEN-
sity of Gabriel's passion and her own. Maybe that explained
what she'd just seen in the window. The beautiful, strangely
familiar blue-eyed man who'd been watching her and Gabriel
on her balcony. The one who'd disappeared.

"You okay, angel?"

Was she? She allowed Gabriel to pick her up and carry her
into the bathroom without protest, feeling a little raw and dev-
astated by what had just happened on the table . . . and then in
the kitchen.

She'd known. He'd kissed her, touched her, before. She'd
come at the thought of him, at the dream of what being with
him would be like.

That wasn't just sex. Not for her. Angelique was no inno-cent. She'd had no-strings sex before. Even great no-strings sex that she'd walked away from with a smile and no regrets. That wasn't what this had been. She'd lost herself in him, in what he had done to her. Given more than her body.

He lowered her to her feet and turned the shower taps, giv-ing her a chance to study his back. Gabriel was a beautiful man. His body was perfectly sculpted, lean and muscular. He turned toward her and she realized his face had filled out in the last few weeks. He looked healthier, stronger, though his expression was still stark, his stare still haunted. Except when he was looking at her.

His green eyes drew her in, such a powerful pull it felt al-most like she wanted to leave her body and melt into him. It was . . . strange.

She lifted her hand to her temple and swayed, suddenly tired.

Gabriel reached for her, pulling her close. "Angelique? You're scaring me, baby. What's wrong?"

"A little fuzzy, but I'm okay." She didn't want him to leave. Didn't want this to end. "I think every muscle in my body turned to Jell-O. Maybe you were right about me not being able to keep up with you," she joked. "Or maybe I just need a shower and a post-nookie snack."

His lips quirked, but his gaze was still alert and watchful. "Then let's take care of you, angel. Because I'm nowhere near done with you yet."

Yet. The word had a new ominous tone. But she wouldn't

think about why. Not tonight. She smiled as he lifted her into the shower and joined her beneath the hot spray.

She closed her eyes, loving the warmth of the water, the gentleness of his hands on her skin as he began to wash her.

His touch was making it hard to concentrate on the man she'd seen just as her last orgasm crashed over her. Gabriel had been relentless in pleasuring her, unwilling to stop until she'd come again, this time in his mouth.

Seeing the stranger had thrown her for a heartbeat, but then she'd known. This was the "something" around Gabriel that his family was worried about. The being they couldn't see, couldn't quite sense.

Why had it shown itself to her?

She turned around to ask him, to confront him about the vision and his family's concerns, but her eyes strayed downward and the words stalled in her throat. His erection stood out from its nest of soft, dark curls, the shaft flushed with color. Thick and long. So hard . . . again.

He obviously hadn't been exaggerating about his stamina or his skills. The memory of how he'd filled her, the tight fit that had driven her crazy, was enough to wake her from her daze. She needed to taste him. Needed to know how the head of his cock felt against her tongue.

She dropped to her knees before he could stop her, grinning up at his concerned expression. "Don't worry. I'm feeling better now. But I'm still a little hungry."

The soapy water swirled past her knees as understanding darkened the green of his eyes. His motions stilled, blocking her from the water's spray while he waited to see what she would do. She lowered her chin until she was eye level with the object of her desire.

He was well endowed, but it didn't intimidate her. It made her impatient. Greedy. She lifted one hand to the thick base of his shaft, fascinated by his texture. The veins and ridges, the marble hardness covered in velvet flesh.

She closed her fingers around as much of him as she could and heard him make a low sound of approval when she leaned forward and licked the tip of his cock with a featherlike, teasing stroke.

Her mouth closed over the head of his erection, teeth scraping gently, tongue swirling over his flesh. Loving his flavor, she hummed in approval. Earth and man, salt and heat. Her chocolate addiction took an instant backseat to the succulent Gabriel.

He swore and his hips tensed, as though he were holding himself back. But she didn't want him to have control. She never had any when he touched her. Fair was fair.

She took more of him into her mouth, sucking in her cheeks as she absorbed more of his taste, feeling him swell further against her hand and mouth as she caressed him. She knew she was tormenting him, teasing him, with slow movements and light licks. Her other hand came up to cup the tight sac between his thighs, cradling him gently. Too gently for him, she knew.

Gabriel gripped a handful of her hair, the curls heavy with water now falling in sodden ropes down her back. He growled. "Angelique." Her name was a rasped warning, showing her how much she was affecting him.

Her tongue wrapped around his shaft, lapping at it like candy. She gripped him tighter, her fist making a slight twisting motion on his smooth, hot erection. His hips pumped jerkily against her, and she tasted the salty tang of arousal on the tip of his cock. She pulled back, her touches lighter once more, knowing it would make him crazy.

"Playtime is over, baby. I can't take it." Gabriel tightened his fingers in her hair tellingly. "Suck me with that beautiful mouth. Take more."

Her eyes watered as his hips began short, shallow thrusts, stretching her mouth wide as she struggled to take more of him. Yes. She wanted this. Wanted this side of him. The carnal words, the domination. He made her want all of it. Everything.

Somehow he knew. "Good girl. That's right, angel. Open wide for me. Take every inch and suck it . . . harder. Fuck, Angelique, your mouth—"

His other hand was in her hair now as he guided her. There was no force—there didn't need to be because she was more than willing. Her body was trembling, feeling empty and aching. She wanted him inside her again, to feel his insistent desire, despite her overwhelming reaction to it.

She breathed out and lowered her head, feeling the head of his cock hit the back of her throat. It was almost too much, but she still tried to take more. Loving his instantaneous reaction.

He moaned, his hips pumping against her. Less controlled now as his own passion took over. Her hips were rocking, too, needing relief, but unwilling to stop until she'd made him come.

She could hear him softly coaxing her beneath his breath. "Yes, baby. Suck it . . . Suck my cock with that hot, sweet mouth . . ."

The hand on his testicles squeezed at the same time she swallowed against his flesh and he shouted out her name. The rich tang of his come filled her mouth as he reached his climax. "Angel. God, it feels . . ."

She couldn't stop shaking. He slipped his softening shaft out of her mouth and she let him go, wrapping her arms around her waist, trying to get her body under control.

Had that act ever worked her up to this degree of arousal? Ever had her longing to take him in her mouth again? To beg for him to take her again? To take her now?

Before she realized what was happening, Gabriel had turned the water off, wrapped her in a towel, and was carrying her toward the large bedroom at the end of the hall.

"Wait."

His green eyes intense, he looked down at her and she shook her head. "My room." She gestured toward the closer door.

She couldn't take him into the master bedroom. She was kinky, but not that kinky. That had always been her mother's room.

Gabriel lifted one dark brow, but followed her directions in silence. He shouldered the door open and stopped, gazing around her room.

She looked around, too, trying to see it through his eyes. It was the room of the youngest Rousseau, the princess of her family. The queen-sized bed was draped in an ivory quilt edged with lace. Framed black-and-white pictures, several of blues singer Bessie Smith, as well as—she blushed—one or two posters of her favorite boy band, still hung on her walls.

"Cute."

Angelique blushed. "I wanted to *be* a singer until I discovered boy singers. Then I just wanted to be a groupie. I leave all the real singing to Kelly now. It's safer for everyone that way."

Gabriel grinned as he absently caressed her bare legs with his fingers. "Good to know. If Mama's stories are any indication, I wanted to build things."

If. She recalled what she'd learned about his childhood. He'd been so young when he was taken away, he didn't even remember his dreams. What he wanted to be when he grew up. It suddenly seemed insensitive for her to bring him here. Regardless of her absentee father, she'd known real love here. The kind of love he'd been starved for.

"Maybe we should—"

"Maybe you should get ready for payback, angel."

She swallowed. "Payback?"

He smiled wickedly as he walked over to the edge of her bed and dropped her still-damp body onto the mattress.

"For all the teasing. For making me crazy." He showed her the foil-covered condom before setting it on her nightstand. Where had that come from? Had he brought one into the bathroom? Talk about being prepared.

He spoke again, drawing her attention back to his words. "For breathing in and out and not knowing how distracting your breasts are when you do. Pick one."

"I didn't tea—" Okay, she did, but not for long. What was he up to?

He came to sit down beside her, adding to the damp mess her bed was becoming, and patted his thighs. "Come over here and take your punishment."

Punishment. Did he mean what she thought he meant? "Now? Here?" Was he a machine? Didn't he know about cuddling?

She studied his stirring body and decided he didn't, but she wasn't sure how she felt about his request. She'd always joked about spanking and being tied up. The idea was alluring, in theory. In practice she'd always imagined she would much rather be the one in control.

Until Gabriel. He brought out a side of her she hadn't known was there.

"The more you make me wait, the harder it will be."

She glanced pointedly at his lap and he chuckled. "That, too. Lie across my legs. On your stomach."

Her dubious expression made his eyes sparkle. "You asked for it." He reached for her before she could move away, turning her semi-reluctant body until it was right where he wanted it: her breasts pressed against his thigh, her ass in the air.

"I've wanted to spank you, for one reason or another, since you told me off in the garden. I've wanted to do more than that." His voice was low and intense. He wasn't pretending. This wasn't play for him. Was this what he liked to do with other women?

She wriggled against him. "Had a lot of practice at it?"

"More than you want to know." His grip tightened on her when she instinctively moved away. "You asked, angel. Not me. I didn't grill you about all the boys you'd practiced on to get so good at sucking cock, did I?"

She flinched. "I forgot for a minute what a jerk you can be."

His voice was grim. "And I forgot what an innocent you are. Maybe too innocent to be spanked at all."

Every part of Angelique rejected his words. She wanted what he did, and despite her tough talk, her heart was racing, expectation making it hard for her to breathe. "You wish."

She thought she heard a whispered, "Good girl," before the sounds and sensations that followed the first cupped blow to her backside replaced coherent thought.

The stinging turned to heat on her skin and adrenaline rushed through her body. The heat spread, and with each carefully aimed, perfectly timed tap on her flesh, it grew.

"Oh!" She shouldn't like this. His hand landed with a loud smack and her eyes watered. She shouldn't, but she did.

The arousal from earlier came back, stronger than before. She'd had no idea it would feel this good. Her body became attuned to his movements. As he quickened his pace, the palm of his hand marking every inch of her sensitive backside, her hips lifted to press against his hand. God, she was shameless.

Her legs spread and she sighed when the cooler air soothed her heated sex, offering momentary relief.

Gabriel groaned. "Your body knows, doesn't it? Knows it was made for this. All these soft curves and golden flesh designed to be pleasured and fondled and fucked."

She couldn't respond beyond a pleading moan when his fingers slid along the seam of her ass until they were drenched in her need. Two thick fingers dipped in and out in time with the motion of her hips. But it wasn't enough.

"Please."

Her head was spinning again, although she wasn't certain whether it was from his touch or the fact that he was repositioning her, moving her until she straddled his lap.

His rough thighs burned against her tingling butt cheeks. She heard the sounds of the condom, knew he was protecting her, but she couldn't see through the haze of arousal. All she could hear in her head, over and over, was *now. Please. Now.* No matter how many times she'd come in the last few hours, she was desperate for more.

"Eventually I'm going to be able to take it slow with you. Take my time."

She looked into his eyes as he lowered her onto his cock. Deeper. Even deeper than before, she thought in wonder, her body arching as every cell reacted to the invasion.

Before lust took over completely, Angelique sent out a secret wish that "eventually" would take a very long time.

Preferably forever.

"ARE YOU *WHISTLING*? OR HAVE I ACCIDENTALLY POPPED back into a different dimension where my assignment isn't an asshole?"

Gabriel continued scrambling the eggs, focused intently on the one meal he knew how to cook. "Go away."

Behind him, Emmanuel huffed out a laugh. "Nope. I'm in the right place. But you do look different. Had a good night, have we?"

Gabriel smiled. "Not sure about you, but *I* did."

A great night. Best sex of his life, if anyone was keeping score. Angelique was . . . Well, she inspired the hell out of him. Every time he'd fulfilled one fantasy, he looked at her and his mind conjured ten more to take its place.

He couldn't remember the last time he'd woken up in such a good mood. The last time he'd slept so well, free of the incessant nightmares that had plagued him for the last year.

Though the dream he'd *had* was strange. Only one shadowy figure had followed him, and it wasn't the *djab*, but something nearly as ominous. He'd woken up just enough to feel Angelique's body cuddle close to his in her sleep, and all his worries had disappeared.

It was disconcerting, the way she did that.

"Your eggs are burning."

Gabriel swore and pulled the small frying pan off the stovetop. Angelique was still asleep, and he'd wanted to wake her with the delicious aroma of eggs and coffee, not an apartment on fire.

He turned on the vent above the stove and opened the cupboard to grab a plate. He paused when he looked at it. A colorful, if oddly shaped, rainbow and what Gabriel thought might be a dog or chicken decorated the dinnerware. The plate beneath it held another image, this one of a giant smiling sun, complete with gapped teeth and sunglasses.

A familiar ache returned to his heart as he studied the evidence of a proud mother and happy children. He'd hardly ever eaten with his father, but when he had, it was servants who set the table, and the plates were fine china, often embellished with silver or gold gilt. Nothing but the best for the Giodarnos. No laughter. No plaques on the wall saying World's Best Dad or drawings proudly put on display.

This was a world he didn't know. Her world.

He set the plate down and covered the brightly colored image with eggs, his smile gone.

Emmanuel shook his head. "There's the face of doom we all know and love."

Gabriel was no longer in the mood for banter. "Shut up."

"You know, if you want to get control of your abilities, you have to get that chip off your shoulder. You had a bad childhood, blah, blah, blah. Would you like to compare scars? I bet I'd win."

He wanted to argue the point but he couldn't. He knew about Emmanuel's childhood. His death. The long years he waited for someone to solve his and his sister's murders. Bastard.

His own abilities. His affinity for drawing in darkness. He didn't want to think about that. He wanted to go back to Angelique's bedroom and find new ways to make her come. She was sunshine to his shadow. She made him forget what he was. Unfortunately, he'd exhausted her long before he'd had his fill.

He'd been naïve to think one night would be enough. And even more foolish to entertain the notion that he could have much more than that.

"What's this?"

Gabriel blinked, looking through the kitchen entry to see Emmanuel standing over Angelique's coffee table. "What do you mean?" He walked over to him and followed his gaze. "The necklace?"

"There's something off about it. Wrong. Even I can see its darkness. Can't you?"

A sleepy female voice interrupted him before he could look closer. "Talking to yourself again?"

"She's alive." Gabriel smiled and walked over to Angelique. "I was worried I'd overdone it."

Her brown eyes, bleary with sleep, still twinkled. "There are some things worth being sore over."

He leaned down for her kiss. "I like your style, angel."

"Ask her about the necklace. This is bad mojo; there's no reason she should have it. Ask her where she got it." Emmanuel's command was sharp, drawing Gabriel's glare.

"What's the blue-eyed cutie bothering you about now?"

Gabriel's head whipped around and he gripped her shoulders a little too tightly. "What did you say?"

"Aha!" She pulled away, pointing at him. "I can see it on your face. I'm right. You *are* talking to someone, aren't you? Someone not even your sister can see. How is that possible? Can't she see all spirits?"

"Listening at keyholes again?" he snapped. Remembering

where Bethany had taken her the day before, he turned to Emmanuel. "She probably got it at the voodoo shop."

Angelique rushed past him and picked up the necklace. "Don't talk about me as if I'm not here." She raised her voice. "To someone too afraid to show himself, no less."

Emmanuel started to reach for her but stopped himself. "She shouldn't have that, Gabe. Especially in the weak state you put her in."

"The state I put her in?" Gabriel snarled, unsure why he was so angry, and whirled on Angelique. "What are you doing with something like that? Did the Mambo send you home with a spell to snare her problem child? I didn't think she worked those kinds of spells. Or was Bethany in on it? Did she send me over here to help you discover what's on everyone's mind?" He threw his hands up in the air. " 'What's wrong with Gabriel? Is he evil or just an asshole? Oh, what can it be? Inquiring, nosy, meddling fucking minds want to know.' "

Angelique stood still, her shoulders unnaturally rigid beneath her long T-shirt that at any other time Gabriel would have found irresistibly sexy.

"If you think that, you should go now."

He didn't want to. The desire to stay was so strong he had to force himself to take one step, then another, away from her. So strong he lashed out. "What? No after-sex cuddle? Not even a blow job for the road?"

"Fuck you."

"Too late." He grabbed his keys and opened her door, feeling no sense of satisfaction as it slammed behind him.

Emmanuel clung to his back like a burr. "Gabriel. Damn it, Gabriel, she doesn't deserve that."

He stomped down the staircase, already regretting what he'd said, and wondering how the morning had gone to hell so quickly. "I blame you. You, this supposed ability I have, *you*, my meddling family." He headed toward his car. "Oh, and you."

A shove between his shoulder blades sent Gabriel stumbling against the car door, and he looked over his shoulder, incredulous. "Did you just *push* me? What are you, *nine*?"

"You're the one acting like a child. More of an ass than usual. You should apologize. You shouldn't leave her alone right now."

He studied Emmanuel. "I'm acting like a child? That's rich. Here's a question for you, oh, wise, ghostly one. How does she know your eyes are blue?"

Emmanuel pressed his lips together, but Gabriel saw something in his expression that made him seethe. "Find your own pussy, Manny. Unless it's me you keep looking at." He smiled mockingly. "That's it, isn't it? You're not following me around because you have some great plan—you just have a crush. Unfortunately I don't swing that way."

The punch took him off guard. It shouldn't have. The really fucking laughable thing was, he was grateful. He deserved it. He'd taken something that had been unbelievable but fragile and smashed it on the ground without a thought.

Jesus, what was wrong with him?

Angelique. He didn't want her to have any ulterior motives for being with him. Didn't want her to know about the darkness that followed him. He'd had a few hours of perfect, and he'd wanted it to last just a little while longer. None of what he was dealing with, what he was, should have touched that perfection. When it had, the part of him that knew exactly how to push people away came out to make someone, anyone, bleed.

He cupped his sore jaw. Emmanuel was right; he should go up there and apologize. On his knees if he had to. He knew her desire for him hadn't been a lie. It was too potent, too raw, to be faked.

But he wouldn't. Maybe it was better this way. It was messy, but she'd figure out quickly, if she hadn't already, that he was not worth the effort. She'd stay away from him. Stay safe. And he'd remember that he wasn't cut out to be in any kind of relationship. It wasn't in his genes.

Emmanuel hadn't left. Gabriel was oddly glad. At least he could do one thing right. "Sorry."

"Me, too."

They got into the car and Gabriel started the engine.

"Gabe, you should know something."

He sighed. What? That he was damned? That Angelique made the sweetest moaning noises when she slept? "I'm sure I should."

"Your 'supposed abilities' affected her."

He straightened. He didn't like the sound of that. But he hadn't seen any darkness around her. "How?"

Emmanuel's tone was somber. "You don't just draw out the darkness."

Gabriel banged his hands on the steering wheel. "That's it.

No more cryptic remarks. No more riddles I need to solve or thugs to fight. If I've—" His voice rasped with emotion. "If I've hurt her, and you could have stopped it—"

"You're right." Emmanuel sounded just as disturbed as Gabriel was. "You're right and they're wrong. *I've* been wrong. The rules no longer apply, not if I'm actually supposed to be helping you. You aren't ready to talk to the Mambo? That's fine. Just go back to Isabel's . . . I mean Bethany and BD's house. We'll tell them everything. Maybe they can help."

Gabriel put the car in drive without another word. Let them think he was crazy, or judge him for what he drew to himself. He couldn't let what touched him hurt Angelique.

He'd never forgive himself.

CHAPTER 10

THE POUNDING REFUSED TO STOP.

Ignore it.

She couldn't. Curled up in one corner of the couch, hugging the pillow she'd stitched for her mother when she was eleven, she listened to the female voices arguing on the other side. Ive and Kelly? She thought they'd gone back to Baton Rouge.

Your friends are gone. If you ever had any. Was Bethany your friend for sending Gabriel?

If she ever had any? Shit, she was maudlin today.

Bethany. After this morning, Angelique had just enough energy to open the envelope she'd sent last night. The one that was so important she'd directed Gabriel to her apartment to

147

hand deliver it. Inside was a single page of paper, with two short sentences.

You're welcome. Be careful.

If the morning had gone differently, Bethany would be her hero. As it was, well, Angelique wished she would have read that last part before she'd kissed him.

She heard Ive's worried voice through the door. "Angelique? If you don't bounce your ass over to this door and let us know you're okay, we're calling your mama!"

Her friends weren't gone. They were threatening her with the one thing that could motivate her after wallowing in self-pity for the entire day. "On my way."

She walked past the kitchen and noticed the cold plate of eggs, the one she'd seen after he'd left. He'd made her breakfast, then followed the kind deed up by unleashing an unprovoked verbal attack that had shocked her.

It shouldn't have. Only a child expected to change a bad boy into Mr. Right with one night of amazing, intimate, life-altering sex. And she wasn't a child.

Or so she kept insisting.

She opened the door and was instantly engulfed in a four-armed embrace. As always, their affection and concern were the perfect balm to her blue mood.

Ive planted a loud kiss on her cheek. "Woman, you have no idea how worried we were. Is your phone broken? Didn't you get any of our messages?"

She'd unplugged her phone when it started to ring. "I'm sorry." She dropped her arms and took a questioning step back. "Is something wrong? I thought you'd gone home."

Ive pointed at Kelly. The usually sunny blonde was glancing anxiously around the room. "Kel had one of her feelings. We don't ignore those; you know that. When you didn't answer any of our calls, we had to come over."

Angelique was surprised. She did feel a bit like her heart was breaking but she wasn't in any danger. At least, she didn't think so. "I'm fine. Kel, are you sure it was about me?"

Kelly turned from her study of the room and examined Angelique from the top of her mussed curls to her slipper-clad feet. She'd hardly moved from the couch all day, too busy feeling sorry for herself to do anything else.

Including eat, she realized when her stomach growled.

"Yes, I'm sure. Ive?"

"What is it, Kelly? Another feeling?"

Kelly shook her head, her expression deadpan. "No. More fact than feeling. I think Angelique had a party without us."

Ive smirked, obviously catching her friend's train of thought. "What kind of party would that be?"

They both looked at her expectantly, waiting for her to finish their running gag. Angelique rolled her eyes. "A pity party."

Ive slipped her arm through Angelique's, leading her into the living room. "You know you never have that kind of party alone, *bebe*. There's planning involved. A few of your closest friends, some chocolate, some liquor . . . maybe a night of no-strings sex with the hottest man you know to blow off some steam."

Angelique's smile faltered. And Kelly noticed.

Her jaw dropped. "Unless you already had sex with the hottest man you know and then he did something to screw it up because he's a man and that's what they do."

A tear slipped down Angelique's cheek and she laughed in surprise, wiping it quickly away. "Who needs empaths and invisible voyeurs when you have best friends?"

Ive's expression was compassionate and protective. "What did that nasty Gabriel do? You know how well I know the male anatomy. I can kick it or I can snip it." She made a motion that had Angelique grin unwillingly. "*Nobody* is allowed to make you cry. Not on my watch."

For some reason, her words turned on the waterworks. Angelique hadn't realized how much she needed her friends until they were there. She loved her family, she truly did, but she would always be the baby to them. Celestin would always fight to protect her and pat her on the head when he was proud. Her mother would always coddle her and lecture her and make excuses for her. None of them would ever share their burdens with her as if she were an equal.

Kelly and Ive were the two people in the world who saw her for what she was now. Who would fight for her and never judge her for her mistakes. They had her back.

"I don't know why I'm such a mess."

Because you know he hates you.

She shook her head, wishing she could remove her morbid thoughts. Wishing she could focus. "We both said it was just sex. But it wasn't . . . He was wonderful and then he was a creep, so I told him to go." She buried her face in her hands, her words muffled. "But he made me breakfast."

She could hardly hear Ive over her pounding headache. "We understand, hon."

"We do? I'm not sure I got *any* of that. I can't even tell if she had 'just sex' or not."

Angelique lifted her head and glared at Kelly. "Yes. Great sex. The best sex in the history of the sport. Everywhere, on everything, all night long. Okay? Satisfied?"

Kelly fanned herself. "No, but you obviously were. So why are we mad at him, again?"

"Because she's falling in love with him." Ive's melodic voice changed Kelly's expression.

"Oh. That makes sense."

It did? She was? Damn it. "Then I need to fall out right now." She sat up straight and sniffed. "Are you two all New Orleansed out?"

Kelly rubbed her hands together. "Never. What's your plan?"

Angelique looked around the apartment and sighed. "I can't stay here anymore. I'm turning into a cliché. I say we get a hotel suite in the middle of the action and see what kind of trouble we can stir up. My treat."

Ive nodded, and the burnished curtain of burgundy hair shimmering in a shoulder-length bob framed her serene smile. "Sounds perfect. But I have one condition."

At her questioning glance Ive's expression turned playful. "Shower, *bebe*. And put on something sexy so we can grab one of the brokenhearted men you'll leave in your wake tonight."

Angelique smiled thankfully and got to her feet. "I'm so glad you're here."

She stepped into the bathroom and her smile disappeared. In her mind she could see Gabriel in the shower, washing her with gentle, loving hands. Gabriel looking down at her kneeling form, begging—no, sensually demanding—her to take more of him into her mouth.

She studied herself in the mirror. Where was sassy, ballsy Angelique Rousseau? The one who knew she was sexy, knew she was worthy? Who was this mess in her place?

If this was what happened when you fell in love, she now knew why she'd avoided it for this long. It was hell on your ego, it hurt a lot, and if your feelings weren't returned? No amount of chocolate or liquor could fix that Shakespearean tragedy.

You could make him love you. Make him need you. Like your father did.

She would rather die. She couldn't believe the idea had entered her mind.

She sent herself a stern expression. Even if she knew how, she never would. If Gabriel didn't want her, or, at least, not enough to treat her the way she deserved, she would deal with it and move on.

There were plenty of kissable frogs around. Not many who could make her feel the way Gabriel did, but there must be one or two who could come close.

You know that's a lie. He's the only one.

For once, unfortunately, she and her gloomy inner voice were in agreement. Hell.

She reached up to run a hand through her hair and heard a light, musical sound. Her fingers opened to reveal a silver chain with the locket she'd taken from Mambo Toussaint's shop dangling from the end.

The ruby gem shone beneath the fluorescent light. It was so beautiful. But she really needed to take it back to the Mambo's.

Strange. She hadn't realized she'd picked it up again.

"FASCINATING."

Gabriel glanced up at Emmanuel in disbelief before returning his gaze to the ex-Loa. "That's it? I've told you everything. Trusted you. Let's recap, shall we? I'm talking to and can see a grown-up non-ghosty version of the brother of your wife's past life." He made a face. He couldn't believe he'd actually just said that. Again. "I've told you about the shadows. That they're drawn to me. If you and my invisible buddy are to be believed, they can even enter me and turn me into a version of the Incredible Hulk of the Big Easy. Or at least a black-eyed, ironfisted wild man. Now, according to Manny, I might have the extra-special talent of unconsciously sucking up souls like a damned energy vampire." He took a deep breath, studying BD's mysterious expression with frustration. "All of that, and *fascinating* is all you've got for me?"

Emmanuel grumbled from his perch on the kitchen island.

It was obvious he was expecting more as well. "Maybe we should have gone to the Mambo's after all. Not sure why I thought Marcel could help."

BD tilted his head. "I don't go by that name anymore. You know that. You haven't forgotten I can hear you, have you, Manuel?"

"Only because I want you to."

BD grinned with true affection. "Neat trick, little brother. Emmanuel, all grown up and alive. Well, not dead—is that what you said? Wish I could see what *that* looked like. Is that my old mentor's doing?"

Emmanuel's jaw tightened. "No. Legba wouldn't have done this."

Gabriel wasn't sure why Emmanuel had refused to show himself. His concession to let the others hear him was all he was willing to agree to. "For now," he'd said.

Emmanuel made a sound of frustration. "I wasn't told very much about why Gabe can do what he can do. Just that I had to get him to find the answers. And bring him home so he could learn to use it. I thought you might know. You were at the crossroads longer than I was. I spent most of my time . . . elsewhere."

BD's expression turned thoughtful. "You know you're just making me curious, yes?" He paused. "They never tell you anything they don't have to. Not even when they're trying to help. It's just their way. And a habit you've obviously acquired. But I told Gabriel the truth the other day. I don't remember everything." He paused. "I do know I thought it was strange, even as a Loa, that the twin of a *bon ange*, the child of such an honored mambo, had his gifts withheld from him. But what he can do now? I'm not sure what that is. In fact, if I were still a Loa, I believe Gabriel's ability would make me wary."

Wary? Gabriel's eyebrows lowered in confusion. Loas were voodoo's version of angels and saints. Immortal and powerful. He would make *them* nervous?

A feminine voice drifted into the room. "Obtenebration."

"Speaking bookworm again, my love? Sounds kinky."

Bethany made a face at her husband as she walked into the kitchen. The moment Gabriel had started explaining what he'd been seeing, her eyes had glossed over. He'd thought she didn't believe him. When she'd disappeared, he'd hesitated, but BD had asked him to continue. Apparently she'd been going to look something up.

"Not that I should be helping, since he didn't tell me all of this as soon as I let him under my roof." Gabriel shifted guiltily at her stare. "It's what Gabriel can do. Well, sort of."

She blushed. "I used to play this online role-playing game. It had vampires . . ."

Gabriel rolled his eyes, growling when Emmanuel whacked his shoulder. "Okay, I'll bite. What is obtenebration?"

She sat down, a large book open in her hands. He'd gotten a glimpse of the cover. He should have known. The answers had been here all along. It had nothing to do with voodoo. No. Instead, all he needed to know could be found in a fictional game about Goth vampires.

"In this context, it means 'the act of darkening' or 'the state of being darkened.'" Bethany bit her lip. "But the, um, characters who have it can pull the darkness in and use it, manipulate it to attack or protect themselves. It's the only reference to what you're describing that I've ever heard of."

"The characters. From the book. About a game."

Emmanuel stood over Bethany's shoulder, his eyes gleaming. "Do not disrespect her. Besides, that sounds right. Or as right as anything can. You did use it to protect yourself, aware or not, the night she found you."

Bethany looked up into the empty space around her, a soft smile tinged with sadness on her face. "The night you told me *where* to find him."

Gabriel saw a flash of vulnerability in Emmanuel's expression and felt a new kinship with him. He'd lost his sister, too. Had the life he'd known taken away from him too soon. Now they were both home, both so close to what they'd wanted. Love. Family. But they were too afraid, or for some reason unable to reach out for it.

He'd been staying away from Michelle. He told himself it was out of shame and fear he would hurt her. He'd left his mother's house for the haven of Bethany and BD's for the same reason. But, he admitted to himself, there was more to it than that.

He had a hard time accepting the love the Mambo offered. He'd held on to his loss for so long, worn it like armor to shield himself from harm. Stop himself from caring about anyone enough to be hurt by them again.

But he hadn't gone far. Gabriel had more than enough money to buy a damn house—hell, ten houses—so why hadn't he? Why had he pushed his way into the home of people who were practically strangers, sleeping on their narrow guest bed and running errands to stay in their good graces?

Because he was selfish. He'd wanted to stay connected to his family. Bethany and BD were that connection. He couldn't let himself trust he could have his family back, but he didn't want to be alone.

What was Emmanuel's reason?

Gabriel rubbed the back of his neck with his palm, thinking of Angelique again. Speaking of hurting people . . . "What about the other thing?"

Bethany's brow furrowed thoughtfully. "You called it soul sucking. Can you be a little more specific? Maybe something like that's in here. How does Emmanuel know you can do that? Maybe if he described what he saw . . ."

Gabriel hesitated, and her blue eyes, so like Emmanuel's, narrowed on him. "How does he know?" she repeated ominously.

"Angelique has a . . . bright soul." Emmanuel had begun pacing. "I noticed it right away." He avoided Gabriel's eyes. "In certain situations, it dims around him. Goes into him. I didn't notice until this morning that he could take too much."

The condemnation Gabriel saw on Bethany's face was no more than he deserved. "I didn't know. God, do you think I would have— She said she was dizzy but I thought—"

BD tapped the table, drawing their attention. "I don't like that phrase, *soul sucking*. I like the name you found. Obtenebration. It sounds omnipotent and menacing. Good name for a superpower."

"We aren't talking about superpowers, my love." Bethany was gritting her teeth. "We're talking about me putting Angelique in danger." She sighed. "Because I'm an idiot. Because I hated everyone telling me to stay away from you and I thought—"

BD reached across the table and took her hand. "No one speaks about my wife that way. Especially now."

Gabriel watched the silent communication between the couple. The love, so obvious even he could recognize it. BD looked at the spunky, bookish woman as though nothing else existed, and Bethany . . . She was looking at BD with an expression he'd thought Angelique had—

No. He wouldn't torture himself.

"Why especially now?" Emmanuel was sitting across from him now, his attention riveted on Bethany.

She blushed. "That's not important." Her eyes widened, as though an idea had suddenly come to her. "Manuel, is it only with her? Have you seen him do that with anyone else?"

Gabriel looked on with interest, and Emmanuel shifted uncomfortably. "Not exactly," he started. "I watched the darker energy gravitate toward him before he was entirely aware of it, and he usually had to find an outlet. Had to fight or . . . other things . . . to dissipate the darkness. This is the first time I've seen him interact with energy when he wasn't . . . well, angry or drunk."

Bethany tilted her head and hummed under her breath. BD laughed. "She's so cute when she does that. It usually means she's figured something out." He lowered his voice conspiratorially. "I find it incredibly arousing. And I always love her ideas. Especially the ones I inspire."

Gabriel shook his head. "What are you thinking?"

"In a way, he did inspire this," Bethany said. "Babe, you told me once there's a difference between spirit and spirits. Or spirit and souls. You said it was something Loas and a few other beings, like Emmanuel, could see occasionally, but something humans could only feel."

BD lowered his long lashes, studying her through them. "Yes. Human beings have souls that come back again and again, but spirit is in and around all life, existing as energy." His eyebrows lifted. "Or emotion."

Bethany beamed at him as if he'd just discovered the cure for the common cold. "Exactly."

Gabriel had a headache. "Can we go back to the role-playing game? That was less confusing."

Bethany turned in her seat, too excited to be still at her discovery. "I don't think anything like a *djab* is following you, Gabriel. I think, just like your sister can see souls—*ghosts*—you can see spirit. The energy or emotions that are around everyone."

"That can't be right." He shook his head. "I see darkness. It's sinister and contagious and ugly."

"That's where you are. Where you've been and where you've drawn your power." BD's voice was soothing, and Gabriel heard the truth in it. "You closed out everything else, and maybe when you did, you blocked your ability to see it."

Were they saying that this was a gift he was born with? Like

Michelle? If so, someone got turned around on their way to delivering it. "This is new. It only happened after I let that demon in."

Emmanuel, who'd been silently listening, grimaced at his words. "You didn't let it in, Gabriel. It took you. You didn't know how to protect yourself from something like that. Nobody could have."

"He's right, Gabriel, and you know it." Bethany laid her free hand on his arm. "And Michelle and your mother know it, too. The point is—"

"The point is you have a superpower, like her book says." BD interrupted his wife and waggled his eyebrows playfully.

Gabriel pinched the bridge of his nose. The man was irritatingly cheerful. "An ability that I have no idea how to use or control, or what the point of it is? One that I've possibly blocked part of and that drives me around the bend?"

"Every hero has his issues." Bethany laughed when he turned in her direction.

Emmanuel caught his eye. "I think BD just wants you to ask what *his* superpower used to be."

Bethany and BD spoke in unison. "Still is."

Lovely. The ex–sex Loa still had only one thing on his mind. "Can we focus on me for a few more minutes? What about Angelique?"

"You don't have to worry about Angelique." Bethany sounded certain.

"He doesn't?"

"I don't?"

She pushed the vampire book in his direction. "You'd have to understand women to know what I'm talking about, and you obviously still have some things to learn. Just read this. Maybe it will give you some ideas about your abilities. Emmanuel, I know you don't want to show yourself, but can I speak with you alone?"

Emmanuel jerked in his seat, then got up to stand beside her. "Of course. I need to speak to you as well."

Before she could disappear, Gabriel reached out to stop her. "Please, Bethany. I don't want to hurt her."

Her expression softened to one of compassion. "Then don't. But I don't think you're taking anything from her that she isn't willing to part with. If I did, I'd have Celestin come over and tackle you. You know that."

He did. "Then . . . ?"

She shook her head. "It's not my place to tell you. Just trust me. And trust yourself. If you don't want to hurt her, you won't."

Emmanuel and Bethany left the room and Gabriel looked down at the book, but he didn't see the writing. He let the relief wash over him. He hadn't hurt her.

He *had* hurt her by being stupid and cruel, but that could be fixed. If he wanted it to be. He thought about how he'd felt waking up with her lying next to him. God, he wanted it to be.

"I've got an idea."

Gabriel glanced at BD suspiciously. "Why do I have the feeling I should be nervous?"

BD held out his arms and shrugged carelessly, but there was something in his eyes that belied his body language. An intensity that made Gabriel focus. "Don't listen, if you like, *mon ami*. But I think you came to me for a reason. And you were right, of course, because I think I am uniquely qualified to help."

"This I have to hear." Gabriel leaned back in the chair and crossed his arms.

"Simple." BD was blunt. "You don't care what I think. I'm a scoundrel with a second chance. An angel fallen from grace. A—"

Gabriel felt his head pounding again. "I get your point."

But he wasn't finished. "I'm not your childhood pal who married your sister, or your watchdog." He gestured in the direction of Emmanuel. "Or your lover's older brother, who is, as we all know, a saint among men."

Gabriel felt his lips curving. It was impossible not to like this guy. "You said you could help?"

BD stood up, pushing his chair back. "I need to see what you do firsthand. We have to get you to a bar. Preferably a place with rowdy patrons and overly loud music."

"That makes perfect sense." Maybe he should read the vampire book.

BD leaned forward, his expression saying he wouldn't take no for an answer. "Now that you know what it is you're looking at, you have power. Power you could be more prone to use incorrectly if you don't understand it. If we don't understand it. Think of it as practice."

It did make a twisted kind of sense. If he ever wanted to be out in the world again, to stop hiding, he'd have to learn how to control this—whatever it was.

"I'm in."

The man's smile was blinding, if tightly controlled. "Just what I wanted to hear. Wait here while I tell my wife where we're going."

Gabriel's loud laughter followed his friend down the hall. "How far the mighty angel has fallen."

BD's answer came back without hesitation. "Ah, but it is worth it."

CHAPTER 11

"MAYBE THIS WAS A MISTAKE."

"All the best adventures start with that sentence, my friend." BD sent the bartender a smile of thanks and lifted the water he'd ordered to his lips.

Gabriel couldn't get over it. Here he was beside one of the most infamous—previously immortal—rogues of the last century, watching him ignore all the women sidling closer to him, more interested in the band than his new fan club.

"Water, BD? I have to admit, you are shattering your image. With that Saints cap on, you look more like a soccer dad than the infamous Bone Daddy."

BD grinned, his striking, amber eyes alight. "Truly? Thank you, Gabriel. You are a good friend."

Gabriel hadn't meant it as a compliment, but it was obvious that was how it was taken. There was no other explanation. Love apparently made men crazy. How else could he explain it? A Loa with power over men and women alike, a being that could live forever, happily domesticated. And Ben Adair, a man who had been relatively sane and successful, now thoroughly tamed by Gabriel's sister. He didn't know Celestin Rousseau as well, but it was clear that the tattooed, dreadlocked, previously possessed rebel had also fallen victim to the cult of happy wedlock.

He'd been at several of his father's weddings. That was a man in love with love. But even as the bride of the moment walked up the aisle, his father had never seemed as content, as whole, as these men did to Gabriel.

He wondered if he had it in him to feel something that strongly, and an image of Angelique and her dimpled, saucy smile immediately filled his mind.

But could it last?

A nervous female voice shook him out of his reverie. "Can I please buy you a drink?"

He turned on his barstool to see a woman who could easily have graced an issue of *Playboy* staring hopefully at the man beside him. She was focused. And clearly willing. Gabriel may as well have been invisible, but he didn't mind. He sipped his beer, waiting curiously for BD's reaction.

The former kinky cupid set down his glass and stood. "You are too kind, *cher*." He took her hand and kissed it with an old-world air that had Gabriel's eyebrows rising to his hairline.

"You are also beautiful and desirable, and I can see you find me pleasing. Regretfully, I must refuse, since I am joyfully reveling in connubial bliss. However, I have no doubt that you will find the perfect man who will wish to bring you as much ecstasy as I could. Perhaps more. Nothing is impossible."

Gabriel smiled sympathetically at the statuesque stunner's confused expression. "He means he's married. And trust me, I've met his wife; you should probably move on."

She walked away, her shoulders slumped as if someone had kicked her favorite puppy. Several other women who'd heard the exchange followed morosely behind her.

He watched BD sit back down and shook his head. "No wonder Bethany doesn't let you out much. Does this happen everywhere you go?"

"Most of the time." BD shrugged one shoulder, unconcerned. "Bethany teases me about it now. Especially since a local cable channel offered me an insane amount of money to host a show teaching men how to attract the opposite sex."

Somehow Gabriel wasn't surprised. BD on television would be a ratings bonanza. Men would watch to be like him, women would watch, just as they were doing now in the bar, because it *was* him.

He'd never thought about what a Loa did when he was no longer a Loa. BD and Bethany had a nice home, and it was obvious they weren't suffering. It was just as obvious that BD was far more interested in doing laundry and chasing his wife around the house than becoming a part of the working class.

Did Loas have retirement funds?

"I take it you turned them down?" he asked.

BD nodded. "There is no honest way to teach sexual attraction. In the end it's there or it's not. If a man cannot make his woman want him, isn't willing to do anything to discover her wildest fantasies and spend a lifetime making them come true, then he doesn't deserve her."

His words resonated with Gabriel. He wanted to discover Angelique's wildest fantasies. He admitted to himself that he was in over his head with her. Despite his growing belief that she probably never wanted to speak to him again, he wanted her too badly to be casual.

"She would forgive you."

Gabriel jerked in surprise, glancing warily at BD as he took another sip of beer. He pushed it away, the flat taste no longer soothing. "Do you read minds, too?"

BD chortled. "Don't have to. You and I are a lot alike. Two nearly irredeemable bastards who fell for women far too good for us. If Bethany can forgive me for a hundred-plus years of decadence and mischief, Angelique could forgive you for being an asshole."

He hadn't fallen for her. He was just obsessed with her. "It's better this way. For everyone."

BD stared at him intently for a few moments and then nodded, the smile returning to his expression, though wariness remained in his gaze. "Perhaps. It depends on you and which path you decide to walk. Speaking of you, don't you think it's time we did the first experiment? I need to see this for myself. See if it stirs any memories from my . . . previous life."

Shit. His heart began to pound in his ears. All the memories of what he'd been through this last year, running from shadows, blacking out, losing himself—came rushing back.

But it wasn't evil. Not in any coherent sense. At least, if Bethany and her unusual theory were correct.

BD gestured toward the gyrating crowd tonight's popular blues band's performance had drawn. "How does this usually happen?"

"I get drunk and start seeing bogeymen."

"Funny." BD's smile was sardonic. "Concentrate. *Voodoo*'s root means *spirit*, you know. Something Mambo Toussaint could have told you if you'd talked to her about it. There are beings of nature and ancestors, and infusing it all is spirit. It's there, and you have the ability to see it. The way I could. Better than I could if the Marassa Twins had a hand in it. Though why they would dole out that kind of power is beyond me."

Gabriel frowned, thinking about something Emmanuel had said. "Beings of nature? Manny said there were others. Not Loa. He was right?"

"Of course. Though if your next question is if that's what he is, I don't think so. I'm not sure what he is, or why the Mysteries decided to send him back."

BD sounded concerned. For whom? Bethany? Emmanuel?

"You aren't sure of much for an ex-Loa, are you?" He grimaced and shook his head. "I'm sorry. It's just—do you doubt they would? What if it's not from them? What if it's something else?" A curse.

Strange movement in a corner booth distracted Gabriel. A

woman was glaring at a couple on the dance floor in unmistakable jealousy. Around her was a swirling darkness, not fully formed . . . just waiting.

"I see something."

BD leaned closer. "Remember what Emmanuel said. Focus. Study it. Watch how it moves. When it senses you, don't turn away."

Gabriel watched. It didn't take long for him to get that sick feeling in the pit of his stomach. The spinning form stilled, darkened, looking for something. Him.

He watched a part of it separate from the angry woman and slink under the table, between the legs of the dancing throng until it was close to him. Closing in.

Gabriel tensed. "It's coming. What if I black out or hurt someone?"

"I won't let you. You won't let you. You're not lost in self-pity now. Not drunk. Just observe it. If you know how it works, you can control it."

He tried to open his mind. To see energy instead of the priest's depictions of slithering serpents. It was feelings. Emotion. Not as sharp or focused because it was hurt mixed with jealousy instead of the rage or hatred he'd witnessed the other night.

It hovered just out of reach, not coming closer. He told BD his observations, never taking his eyes from it.

"I wonder. The other energy didn't hesitate, did it?" BD asked. "It came for you."

"Yes."

"Why?" BD lowered his voice. "Because you were being attacked? Because you felt it, too? You were angry with the men trying to harm you. Do you suppose like draws like? That you can see it, but draw it only when you allow yourself to feel the feeling that created it?" BD sounded enthralled.

Great. Gabriel was glad someone was enjoying this twisted trip into loony land.

"Gabriel." BD's voice had taken a new, cautious note. "I think we should stop now."

"Why?"

"Because I didn't know she was here."

She? Gabriel tore his attention from the weaving shadow and scanned the crowd. He saw her in the middle of the dance floor.

Her body swayed to a sultry rhythm, arms raised above her head as she lifted her golden-brown curls off her neck. The dress she wore was snug against her thighs. Her breasts strained against the stretching fabric.

Two men framed her, watching the way her body moved, moving with her. She smiled seductively at the one on her right, turning her body until her back was pressed against his front, her ass rubbing against his—

"Angelique."

A burst of energy exploded against his chest. So powerful it knocked the breath out of him. When he looked back at where the shadow had been, it was gone.

But not far.

He could feel the darkness now, fueled by his own jealousy

at the sight of Angelique on the dance floor. Muddling his thoughts. Making him think of all the ways he would kill the man who was touching his woman. Who thought he could take her from him.

"Get ahold of yourself." BD was standing in front of him, forcing him to focus. "You said it was jealousy. So we were right. Like draws like. That makes this easier. Understand it, relate to it, but don't let it take over."

It was a difficult command. Nearly impossible. "I have to talk to her." *Have to get her away from those soon-to-be-dead men trying to dry hump her.*

BD hesitated, restraining him with strong hands on his shoulders. "Blue Eyes will probably geld me for going along with you, but I will. Angelique is hurt and probably not think-ing straight. You are definitely not. But sometimes that's when we need each other the most. And I need—we all need answers."

He stepped back and Gabriel launched to his feet, his hands clenched into tight fists as he sought to restrain himself. He studied the man dancing to the left of Angelique, looking down her dress, and imagined punching him in his leering eye.

The stranger's head whipped back and he grunted in pain, reaching for his eye. Gabriel blinked in surprise even as brutal satisfaction filled him. If he hadn't seen it with his own eyes, he wouldn't have believed it.

No one else had seen the shadow that had done what Gabriel was too far away to do, but BD noticed the result and winced.

"Superpower, indeed. Not exactly restraint, but better than the alternative." He kept his voice calm as he followed Gabriel through the crowd. "If you're listening to my advice, I'd say no to violence, and yes to showing the girl how much you want her. Don't lose control."

Control. He had to keep control. He wasn't weak. He would never allow himself to be overtaken by something again. But that didn't stop him from making a beeline toward Angelique. From being pissed.

He'd been concerned for her all day. Wanting her. Hating himself for causing her pain. Yet here she was, dressed in a come-and-get-me dress and picking his replacement.

That was *not* going to happen. If she was hungry for more, Gabriel would be more than happy to oblige.

"Are you sure you don't want to go back to the hotel, hon? We can order room service. Anything you want."

Angelique ignored Kelly's offer and stood by her seat, her body swaying to the music. She knew her friends were worried about her, but they were bringing her down.

"I'm going to get another drink." She turned, taking only a few steps into the crowd when she bumped into someone. "Excuse me."

"Thought you might like that drink now."

It was that man. The same creepy drunk from the bar the other night. What was he doing here? "Are you following me?"

He towered over her, his smile still cruel. "I told you, didn't I? Warned you? But we can still fix it . . . if you agree to walk away from the Dark Messenger like a good girl."

A good girl. In all his insane babbling that was what she heard. That was what everyone thought she was.

You're not. You aren't good. How can you be? You're a Rousseau.

She poked the man in the chest, heedless of his size. "Look, buddy, I don't want a drink from you, I don't want to dance, and I do not need one more person telling me what to do. I know you're a little crazy with the rum, but do you get that?"

He stepped back, his smile disappearing. "Your choice."

She pushed past him and made her way to the end of the bar, gesturing to the bartender. She was still irritated when she arrived back at her table, her hands full of margarita. "You would not believe what just happened to me. Here, take one of these."

She tried to hand a chilly glass to Kelly, but she refused. "I'm fine with my water, hon."

Angelique sighed. "Wasn't it just a few days ago that you two got me drunk, paid for a lap dance, and had me nearly breaking and entering the house of a family friend with no thought to the consequences? Were you changed into sticks-in-the-mud overnight?"

She set down the drinks and took a breath. That was rude. She probably shouldn't have worded it like that.

They're jealous of you. They want all the attention for themselves.

They were a little high maintenance on occasion, true. But she'd never seen better friends, and they always put her first.

God, she had a headache. "Come on, I thought we came here to have fun. Look—margaritas!"

She and Kelly and Ive had gotten to the hotel, made one another up, and headed out in search of a good time. The music had called to her. So much so, she hadn't been able to sit down once since she got here. But, other than her run-in with Mr. Weirdo, she had been enjoying herself. Enjoying her drinks. More than usual.

Ive and Kelly, for once, were not.

Who cares about them? You can make any man want you. Make any man kill for you.

Where were these thoughts coming from? Her hand came up to fiddle with her necklace, and her fingers slid over a warm, oval locket instead. She held her breath until she felt the tiny cross that sat at the base of her throat. Her touchstone.

Why had she put the locket on? It was beautiful, but not exactly something she'd thought to wear. Still, she hadn't wanted to leave it behind. It might have been stolen or lost.

She had to keep it close. At least until she could get it back to Gabriel's mother.

"Angelique, you are freaking me out. Will you sit down, please?"

Ive put a warning hand on Kelly's arm, but Kelly pulled away. "No, Ive, you know I'm right. She's acting strange. She's barely looked our way, and when she has it's been . . . off. I have a bad feeling."

Angelique rolled her eyes, a dark emotion welling up inside her. "So much for solidarity. *I'm* acting strange? This from the person who lets her *feelings* make all her life decisions . . . when she makes any at all. It's a good thing Ive is a pushover for lost causes."

She saw Kelly's shattered expression, the anger in Ive's usually serene expression, and sat down, her arms reaching across the table toward them. "Shit, I'm sorry. I didn't mean it. Not a word. I love you both more than family—you know I do." Their hesitation almost broke her heart. "Kelly, I love how special you are. And you're always right, always full of life and looking for the next adventure. And Ive *is* a sucker for lost causes. All the greatest doctors are. Which hopefully means she'll forgive me if I beg and swear to never drink another margarita again?"

Ive held out her arms and Angelique flew out of her chair, sliding into the long, booth-like seat between them. "I don't know what I'd do without you two."

Kelly leaned her head on Angelique's shoulder. "We still have a room for you if you want to come back to Baton Rouge, you know. Maybe being near family and . . . other people isn't good for you."

She came close to crying in relief. "Maybe you're right."

She'd come back to see which path she'd take, but since she'd been here, all she'd done was confuse the issue. Gabriel was a giant knot she didn't think she could untangle. And if he was staying here, maybe she should get away. Back to where she knew who she was and what she really wanted.

Hopefully it wasn't too late.

She leaned her head back. "I feel edgy. I need to work off some of this tension." She rolled her head on the leather back of the seat and looked into Kelly's forgiving gaze. "Will you dance with me?"

Kelly's smile wavered, but it was there. "I don't know. This might be too much sexy for you to handle."

"Oh, I can handle your sexy." Angelique waggled her eyebrows.

Ive chuckled. "Sassy. The both of you."

The three women rose together and, holding hands, headed out to the crowded dance floor. As the thundering beat pounded out an addictive cadence that Angelique could feel to her toes, she started to move. Through loving eyes she watched her friends move to face her, swaying in time to the rhythm she'd set.

This was what she needed. No men. No distraction. Just this. Ive did one of the moves she'd learned in her belly-dancing class, and Angelique and Kelly roared in approval, trying desperately to follow her.

Tears of laughter fell from Kelly's eyes as Ive and Angelique moved to sandwich her between them, none of them noticing that the crowd had made a small space for them on the dance floor, watching the women dance.

Kelly spoke in Angelique's ear. "Now, this is a party."

Angelique pulled her close, still moving to the beat. "I love you, you know."

There was a smile in her friend's voice. "I know. I love you, too."

"Good. I was worried for a second I might lose you to the hot guy with long hair behind you."

Kelly pulled back, eyes wide as she tried to discern the truth from Angelique's expression. The man behind her placed a questioning hand on her shoulder. She turned, looking up at the six-foot-and-then-some handsome, bearded hunk. "Yes?"

"Will you dance with me?" The man's voice was deep and gentle. Sexy.

Kelly looked over her shoulder, and Angelique nodded. "Have fun. I'll be here."

She turned to find Ive paired up as well. That was fast. But it always happened. They always attracted attention when they were together, in one way or another.

One song blended into the next, and Angelique knew she wouldn't stop dancing. She couldn't. Something about the beat was hypnotic. She closed her eyes and let it take her. Without being able to help herself she saw Gabriel in front of her, watching her dance just for him. His eyes said, "Seduce me."

So she did.

Bodies closed in around her, but that was a part of the fantasy. She would tempt him by showing him what he was missing.

Angelique smiled up at the handsome stranger beside her and let him tug her backward, rocking against him. Against Gabriel. He wanted her again. No one but her. And nothing would stop him from taking what he wanted.

"Don't mean to disturb you, little Rousseau. I just found a new partner for your dancing buddy."

Her eyes popped open, the illusion bursting at the sight of BD standing in front of her, his smile not reaching his eyes. She watched in shock as he tugged her to his side, handing the man she'd been dancing with over to a tall, blonde bombshell. "I'm sure you two will have amazing sex. I can tell. It is what you might call my superpower. Enjoy."

With that he began to walk off the dance floor through the mass of bodies, her hand still in his. "Wait. What are you doing here?"

BD shouted over her shoulder. "Saving that poor man from an untimely demise. And you from yourself."

"What?"

He ignored her, speaking to someone in front of him. "See? I found her. No harm done. We can all relax."

She leaned around his body and gasped. "Gabriel?"

He stood so still at the edge of the dance floor that for a moment he looked inhuman. A statue. Until she saw the tick at his temple and the clenched fists at his sides. He was upset. Wait. What did he have to be mad about?

"What's going on, BD? Why are you hanging out with *him*?" And where was BD's wife? Angelique was thinking she might have a thing or two to say to her after her botched attempt at matchmaking.

Hopefully BD wasn't trying to follow in her footsteps. She was not in the mood tonight, no matter how mouthwatering Gabriel looked.

Gabriel stepped around BD until he was close enough to touch. So close she had to crane her neck to meet his gaze.

His silence was making her crazy. Why was he looking at her like that? Like she'd been unfaithful. Like she'd done something wrong.

"Did you forget something this morning, Gabriel? Any other insults or accusations you want to hurl at me before you leave me the hell alone?"

She wanted to kiss him. How dysfunctional was that? Despite his obvious anger, she could see something in his eyes, something she wasn't willing to put into words, something she wasn't able to believe.

He wants you. Use that. He'll be lost to lust. Then you'll have him.

No. It wasn't enough anymore. It hadn't been from the moment he'd touched her. She wasn't able to keep her heart out of the equation.

BD laid a hand on her shoulder, ignoring Gabriel's low growl. "We didn't know you were here, *cher*. I promise. Gabriel and I were just . . . talking."

"It's okay, BD." She couldn't look away from Gabriel. She lifted her chin, trying to hide the arousal rising inside her. "I was about to leave anyway. Actually, I think I'm heading back to Baton Rouge. This city is getting too small for me."

She'd barely finished her sentence when Gabriel's hands shot out from his sides, dragging her up against his body. "You aren't going anywhere."

Angelique's body started to tremble, instinctively recognizing him, remembering how he made it feel. "You have no control over what I do. *Just sex*, remember?"

"Hey, where are you going with her, you . . . um . . . you . . ."

Angelique managed to tear her gaze away from Gabriel long enough to see a breathless Kelly stop dead beside them, Ive close behind.

Good. Reinforcements had arrived before she lost her perspective.

BD took a step closer to her two friends. "Ladies. You must be the friends from college I've been hearing about." He lowered his voice. "I'm Bone Daddy."

Angelique's shoulders slumped. The turncoats. Three little words and they turned to putty in his hands, forgetting all about their endangered friend.

"Of course you are. She was right. You're pretty." Kelly sounded like someone had knocked her over the head with a sledgehammer. Although she could be mistaken. Pressed up against Gabriel's body, feeling his heartbeat, smelling him, was making it harder and harder to think.

Gabriel's fingers tightened on her shoulders. "You're coming with me, angel. Now."

She looked up at him, hearing her friends' protests, but she knew it was too late. Of course she was going with him.

You can't resist. How easy you are to control.

Tell her something she didn't know. No matter how bad she knew it would be for her, she couldn't stop her body's reaction. Or her heart's.

"Beautiful ladies, please." BD interrupted Ive and Kelly's argument behind her. "I think we should let them sort it out. Tell you what—I'll buy you both something to drink and tell you how Bone Daddy, a simple Loa, managed to bring together three of the greatest love matches of the centu—oomph. Excuse me, sir . . ."

Angelique held her breath as that strange man pushed past

BD without pause, watched as BD's beautiful amber gaze narrowed in suspicion. "That's an unusual coincidence. And I don't believe in them as a rule."

Ive tilted her head charmingly. "What's a coincidence?"

Gabriel didn't wait to hear his answer. His hands slid down, one of them grasping Angelique's as he turned and started for the door.

She wanted to tell him off. Wanted to get in the car tonight and drive as far away from him as she could. Wanted to feel him inside her again more than anything else.

The cooler air hit her, the blaze of the streetlights breaking her out of her silence. "Gabriel, stop. I—"

He turned, pressing her back up against the brick wall of the club with his body, his lips silencing any denial she might have come up with.

Yes. It felt like years instead of hours since he'd kissed her. It felt like coming home. Or falling off a cliff.

Gabriel reached down to grasp one of her thighs, heedless of the skin revealed as he wrapped it around his waist, letting her feel his erection through the fabric separating them.

She inhaled sharply against his mouth, not caring where they were or who saw them. She just wanted to feel the way she had last night. Just one more time. Maybe then she'd find the strength to refuse him.

His hand came up to cup her breast and she cried out. At the sound he reared back and swore beneath his breath. "Jesus, Angelique, I'm sorry, baby. I don't know if I can wait until we get to the apartment. Fuck, this is insane."

Angelique made a breathless sound of agreement. She was so turned on she could hardly speak. "I know. Don't have to wait. Hotel. One block."

She slipped her hand down between their bodies, rubbing against him. He moaned. Her fingers searched beneath the fabric of her belt until she found what she was looking for. She held the narrow card up victoriously. "I have a key."

Understanding and a relief so profound it mirrored her own crossed over his face. "Thank God."

He half walked, half dragged her down the sidewalk. Angelique supposed she should be glad he hadn't tossed her over his shoulder.

She could hear him muttering under his breath in disbelief at his own behavior. "I wouldn't have cared. I would have taken you up against the wall, in front of everyone."

She knew. Worse, she would have let him.

CHAPTER 12

THE ELEVATOR HADN'T CLOSED TO TAKE THEM TO THE FLOOR her room was on before her back was against the wall and Gabriel's hand was beneath her dress.

In his heart he knew the possessiveness he felt wasn't caused by the shadow that had been drawn to him. It only intensified what had already been there. What he hadn't been able to accept until now.

She was his.

He bit her lower lip, his breathing ragged. "This is for *me*. You're soaking my hand, angel. Say it."

"For you, Gabriel."

He pushed her thin panties to the side and curled two

fingers deep inside her. No teasing. He had to feel her around him. Was aching for it.

But he needed more. He needed to know she was giving him everything. All her passion. Giving up her control to him.

"If I wanted to take you here, you would let me, wouldn't you?"

"Yes, here. Anywhere." She sounded dazed.

His fingers slid out of her wet heat and he brought his hand to her mouth, painting her lips with her own juices.

He licked along the seam of her mouth. "Sweet. Don't space out on me, baby. I have plans."

Her tongue slipped out and followed his, tasting herself as the elevator doors slid open.

Damn, she was responsive. Addictive. Sex incarnate.

Mine.

He placed his hand on the small of her back, taking the card from her and following her to the hotel room she'd gotten with her friends.

Gabriel wanted to ask why she wasn't staying at the apartment. Why she'd worn the scrap of nothing she had on and danced so seductively for other men. But it didn't matter now. She'd come with him.

He opened the door and followed her inside, covering her hand when she reached for the light switch.

"Not yet," he whispered against her ear, loving the way she shivered against him. He reached behind him and bolted the door. Didn't want her friends wandering in uninvited.

The drapes were open and the dim light from the side street

cast the room in shadow. He guided her past the entertainment center, the chair and table. He moved toward the French windows, smiling at the decorative wrought iron he could see on the other side.

She stumbled in hesitation. "The bed is over there."

Gabriel heard his dark chuckle as if from a distance, the blood rushing to his cock making his thoughts cloudy. "Good to know. Next time, I'll use this excuse for a dress to tie your hands to the headboard while I make you beg."

"Oh God."

She was shaking again, but she seemed more energized than weak. Good. He felt powerful and he didn't want to think it was because of what Emmanuel had seen earlier. Maybe it was a combination of proving to himself that he had some control over his strange abilities and her.

Just being with her.

He stood behind her, taking off his shirt while letting her feel his cock pressing against her sweetly curving ass. "This time." He paused, letting her wonder, knowing she was holding her breath, waiting for him to speak. "This time I'm going to give you what you want."

He unzipped his pants, his knuckles purposefully scraping along the base of her spine. She gasped.

"Open the windows, Angelique."

She tensed and started to turn around. "What? No."

He used his body to stop her. His hands on her hips. "No? No, you don't want me to fuck you? No, you don't want to feel that forbidden rush, looking down from this dark room knowing anyone could walk by. Knowing you'd have to be quiet if they did, or they might look up and see you. Look up and know."

He bit his lip so hard he tasted blood as he waited for her to decide. Each second felt like hours. But he waited.

She opened the windows.

"Oh, you are perfect." For him. He slid one hand up to the middle of her back, loving how she curled toward him like a cat.

He bent his head until his lips skimmed her temple. "Now bend over and hold on to those bars."

She moaned, but this time she didn't argue. She was bent at the waist, her breasts pushed down against the narrow swirls of iron that framed the other side of the glass like a miniature balcony. Her fingers curled over the bars; he could see how tightly she gripped, her knuckles going white.

Beautiful.

The move pressed her ass hard against him, and he gritted his teeth, trying to hang on to his sanity long enough to give her what she needed. What she wanted.

He stroked her back through her dress with one hand, reaching in his pocket for a condom with the other. "Someone told me, not that long ago, that to make my woman desire me above all others, I had to find out what her wildest fantasy was, and give it to her."

Her high-pitched "Oh?" made him laugh softly.

"I think I've found one of yours. Shall we test my theory?"

In the darkness of the room he reached for the hem of her dress, lifting it to her waist. She was wearing another lacy thong. This one was black to match her dress. Gabriel slid his fingers beneath the elastic and dragged it over to one side, revealing her to his gaze.

He hummed. "Mmmmm, now I wish I'd let you turn the lights on. This is a beautiful sight."

"Gabriel." His name was a plea on her lips.

"I know." He didn't want to wait anymore.

He slid the condom onto his erection, but the darker forces in his mind were resistant. There should be nothing between them. She belonged to him.

Not yet. The *yet* soothed him enough to allow him to continue. "Anybody below us, baby?"

"I don't, um . . . No."

He held her hips once more and slid his cock between her legs. "Too bad. I know from experience how beautiful you look when I do this."

Gabriel couldn't hold back his groan of pleasure as he filled her with one deep thrust of his hips.

Angelique covered her mouth with one hand, the other gripping the railing for white-knuckled dear life. *Don't scream, don't scream.*

Oh, but she wanted to. So good. She couldn't believe this was happening. That she was bent out the window of her hotel room while Gabriel took her from behind.

It was insane. Probably illegal. The sexiest thing she'd ever experienced. And after last night she'd have thought that impossible.

His hips pumped against her, rocking her, pushing her

barely covered breasts against the rough, aged iron. The chain of the locket and her cross both made the smallest jingling noises, noises that someone on the street could hear if they were listening. It threw her, how erotic it was. How something so illicit could feel this good.

She couldn't close her eyes, couldn't stop them from scanning the street below. When she saw a small group of people, laughing and talking to one another as they walked toward their next adventure, she tensed.

Gabriel leaned against her back gently, looking over her shoulder. His whisper brushed past her skin, its own caress. "I knew it. Felt it. You got wetter. Tighter. You love this. And I love how hot it makes you."

She watched them disappear without looking up, gasping with relief and arousal. Gabriel's hands left her hips, one circling around to slide through her sex, the other going to the low cleavage of her dress, his hips making shallow thrusts that were driving her wild.

"I love your breasts. You know how lush they are. How men stare at them when you're not looking." His rough fingertips traced the flesh over the fabric, and she knew he could hear how fast her heart was beating.

"Most of the time I want to keep them all to myself. Want to be the only one to see them. But I can feel your sweet pussy melting around my cock, know how hard I can make you come . . . so I'm feeling generous."

He tugged her top down, freeing her breasts from the

snug, stretchy fabric. Cool air brushed her sensitive nipples, the feel of steel on her bare flesh nearly making her cry. "Oh my God."

He pushed her hair to one side to get a better view. She felt his lips brush her shoulder as he sighed roughly. "Now, that is what I call a view."

"Please." She tried to keep her voice down, but her body was like one raw nerve. She felt everything. Every sensation. Cold, hot. Pain, pleasure. Fear and hope of being seen. All of them making her ready to beg.

The fingers in her sex tilted her higher against him, his strokes getting deeper. Harder.

"Yes. That. Please do that."

She noticed a glimmer of movement in the shadows on the corner. Two men, around her age. "Oh shit," she whispered harshly.

They were looking right at her.

Gabriel had straightened, hips pumping hard against her as he started to lose his own control. She loved it. She wanted him to fuck her hard. Wanted him to claim her.

The men hadn't turned away. She watched the taller one step closer to the other until he was standing behind him. The smaller man with the spiky black hair went still, his eyes widening in surprise, then pleasure.

Angelique looked down and bit her lip to hold back the sound threatening to escape. The tall man was touching him, cupping him, while they watched her in silent fascination.

The next moment Gabriel picked up his pace, and all Angelique could do was hold on to the bars, arching her back and feeling the weight of her breasts rock with his powerful thrusting.

"They still watching you, angel?" Gabriel's low words were so rough it took her a moment to realize. He knew. He knew she was being watched.

"Yes."

"Then let's show them how pretty you are when I make you come."

He pressed on her clit, thrusting his cock so deep inside her she couldn't stop her short, sharp cry. The iron rattled with the tightness of her grip as her climax shattered her into a thousand pieces. She wasn't sure she'd be able to put them back together. Or if she even wanted to try.

Gabriel's hoarse voice called out her name as he joined her, his damp chest warm against her back as he kissed her shoulder, her neck.

"I don't see anyone."

She looked down, amazed to realize she'd forgotten their audience. Forgotten everything but Gabriel and the way he made her feel.

They were gone. Maybe they'd gone back to their own room. Maybe they'd only been in her mind. She silently thanked them for helping her in fulfilling one of her secret fantasies.

Gabriel wrapped one arm around her shoulders, tugging her back inside the unlit room. "You are one dangerous woman, Angelique Rousseau."

"Yes, she is."

She gasped and spun around in the darkness at the sound of the strange male voice. "I thought you locked the door. Who is that?"

EMMANUEL WATCHED GABRIEL SIGH AS HE REMOVED HIS condom before pulling Angelique back in his arms.

"That's the blue-eyed man I'm always talking to. The one with a lousy sense of timing. Emmanuel, meet Angelique." He looked around, irritated. "This would probably be easier on her if you showed yourself."

He hadn't thought that far ahead. He wasn't sure why he'd let them know he was here. He should have left them alone instead of spying on them again. Though this time it looked as if Gabriel wouldn't have minded.

Angelique yanked up the top of her dress, which was a shame. She was a goddess. A glorious flesh-and-bone goddess. And he *was* a Peeping Tom.

Emmanuel allowed her to see him when she looked like she was appropriately covered, and she jumped in Gabriel's embrace. "You."

He noticed Gabriel's jaw tighten. "You?"

Emmanuel shrugged, slipping his hands in the pockets of his long coat. He knew this already. "I was watching through the window the other night."

Angelique tilted her head. "I thought I saw you; then you disappeared."

"That's what he does." Gabriel lifted one eyebrow. "Any particular reason for this visit, Manny?"

There had been. He was sure of it. He'd wondered how the experiment had gone, though he could see it had taken an unexpected turn.

He wanted to spar with Gabriel so he wouldn't have to think about how difficult his conversation with his sister had been. How he hadn't shown himself to her so she wouldn't see the sadness on his face when she told him what he'd already suspected.

Bethany was pregnant. When she was Isabel, a lifetime ago, she had been like a mother to him. The only person who truly loved him. There'd been a time he'd thought . . . but now another soul, a new soul, would be born into her life. And he was happy for her.

And he felt farther away from her than ever.

He'd asked her about Angelique's locket. Bethany had told him she'd seen Angelique with it and told her to ask the Mambo's permission before taking it. Only Emmanuel knew Mambo Toussaint would never have allowed Angelique to take the necklace. Even a trained hougan or mambo would have trouble dealing with the negative energy that locket was emitting. He'd been surprised Gabriel hadn't seen it more clearly.

Bethany had promised to look through the journals she'd been given. Talk to the Mambo. Try to find out more. He knew she would; she'd always been good at puzzles. Then he'd left without telling her why he'd come. Without telling her he loved her.

"Are you okay, Emmanuel?" Angelique had taken a step

closer to him without him realizing it. Her sympathy radiated off her in waves.

He didn't want pity. Especially from her. She was his. Well— he glanced up at his charge—not *his*. It was clear now she was Gabriel's woman. But she was Emmanuel's Venus. His ideal. He shouldn't let her see him this way.

Before he could speak, Gabriel's voice broke through the silence. "Angelique, do you think Manny here is handsome?"

"Of all the rude—" She turned to look at Gabriel, her expression incredulous. "Why would you ask me that?"

Gabriel studied her, his smile tight. "You're blushing."

Emmanuel wasn't sure what he was doing, but he could see he was upsetting Angelique. "Gabe, stop. She doesn't have to answer that."

"Oh, but she does. You see, tonight is the night we give her everything she wants—isn't it, baby? All her wildest fantasies. A rule is a rule." Gabriel didn't sound like he liked the rule. And Emmanuel still wasn't sure what he was talking about.

He watched Angelique shift from one bare foot to the other, her arms crossing and uncrossing, the expression on her face changing from disbelief, to suspicion, to excitement.

"Do you think he's handsome?" Gabe repeated.

"Yes."

Emmanuel shouldn't feel as good as he did, but he couldn't help it. She liked the way he looked.

Gabriel lowered the timbre of his voice, looking directly into her eyes. "Go to the bedroom, take off your clothes, then sit at the edge of the bed and wait for us."

When she turned and walked directly to the bedroom without argument, Emmanuel felt his jaw drop in shock. That didn't seem like her. "What have you done to her?"

His charge smiled, green eyes darkening with a knowledge Emmanuel didn't have. "Not as much as I want to. Yet."

Together they watched the line of her back revealing itself as she wriggled out of her black dress and underwear, slipping something over her neck and dropping it into the pile before disappearing from view.

Emmanuel took a shaky breath. "What are you up to, Gabe?"

"You want her."

He opened his mouth to deny it but Gabriel shook his head. "That wasn't a question. You've watched us. You've seen her. You'd have to be dead not to want her, and as you keep telling us, you aren't dead anymore. I do have a question, though. You've never been with anyone before, have you?"

Emmanuel ran a hand through the hair at his temple. "What do *you* think, genius?"

"Want to?" Gabriel's face was serious, no threat or artifice in his gaze. Emmanuel still couldn't believe what he was hearing.

"Why are you doing this?"

Gabriel shrugged. "Call it testing my new abilities. I think I still have some jealous energy to work off from the bar. A large part of me wants to maim you just for looking at her, but the more important parts want to please her. Want to give her everything. Anything. Hell, I don't know why."

But Emmanuel knew. He may not know as much about desire, but he knew love when he saw it. And it was changing

Gabriel, making him seem . . . lighter . . . despite his posturing. Had this been a part of the plan all along? No one had told him about Angelique, but then, they hadn't told him a lot of things.

Like how flexible the rules could be. He wasn't supposed to interfere or let anyone else know he was, and yet, nothing had happened when he'd shown himself.

He also hadn't been told how hard it would be to remain on the outside looking in. Something Gabriel seemed to be offering a solution to.

He wasn't sure what to say. He wasn't even sure what he was supposed to do. Could he touch her? The idea sent a tingle of pure excitement up his spine and made his jeans grow uncomfortably tight.

Gabriel gripped his collar. "Just once, Manny. I won't make this offer again. And you have to listen to me for a change."

He could do that. If it meant she could know he was there. That she would know him. He nodded swiftly and Gabriel let him go.

Watching as he headed into the bedroom, Emmanuel followed slowly behind him. A part of him was sure he would be ripped away or struck with a bolt of lightning by the ones who sent him here. This wasn't why he'd come. This wasn't his mission. He was here to guide, to watch, to look after. He shouldn't allow himself to get distracted.

If they wanted to take him, they would. Until then, there was nothing on Earth or the other side that could stop him from walking through that door.

CHAPTER 13

SHE WAS CERTAIN SHE WOULD WAKE UP AT ANY MOMENT.
Then what she'd just done at the window with Gabriel, and the
man who'd appeared in the sitting area of the hotel room, all of
it would make sense. Oh, that was why she'd behaved that way,
she would think. She'd been dreaming.

Only she was fairly certain she was awake. Awake and sitting
naked on the edge of the bed, waiting for Gabriel . . . and his
friend.

Emmanuel. It was too much of a coincidence. Those eyes
and that name. But Bethany had said he was a child when he'd
disappeared with Papa Legba at the crossroads.

She blew out a shaky breath. He didn't look like a child.
He was beautiful. She vowed to herself that she would stop

eavesdropping and asking so many questions from now on. The more she knew about this world BD had opened up to them, this world of voodoo and spirits and magic, the stranger it got. She missed her crazy professor and his "theories." The facts were almost too much for her to handle.

Why was she doing this? The answer came back swiftly. Because Gabriel had told her to, in a voice that instantly renewed her need and heightened her arousal. A voice she felt compelled to obey, because she knew what would happen next. Or, if not what, then how good it would make her feel.

Two men? She thought about the ones she'd seen on the street. They'd been aroused by watching her. They'd touched each other. Somehow she didn't think that was what Gabriel had in mind.

Did he want Emmanuel to watch *them* again, this time without hiding from sight? The thought was exhilarating. What if he wanted more? Ordered her to touch the other man. Kiss him.

He wouldn't. He'd been jealous at the bar. Possessive. He wouldn't want to share her. And even if he did, she wouldn't say yes. Would she?

God, yes.

She couldn't lie to herself. Just the idea of it had her hand slipping down her belly, her thighs shifting as her desire increased. If they didn't come in here soon, she might have to find her own relief, imagining herself between them.

"Someone is looking for another spanking." Gabriel's wicked words sent a shiver up her spine.

Yes, please.

She tried to send him an innocent look. "What? You didn't tell me not to."

They smiled at each other, both knowing that the promise of punishment was no threat. She'd loved it, a fact she'd been unable to hide.

The tall, raven-haired Emmanuel walked into the room, and she froze. Imagining him was one thing; having a fully clothed man see her naked left her feeling vulnerable and un-nerved.

Gabriel knelt in front of her and she was distracted for a moment by his broad, bare shoulders and the open flap of his pants. But then he placed his thumb and finger on her chin, lifting her gaze to his.

"You okay?" His expression was so tender it gave her hope. Did he feel something for her, after all? Was it close to what she now knew she felt for him?

She loved him. Wherever it took her, whatever the toll to be paid. All her talk to the contrary, she didn't want to leave New Orleans. She wanted to stay with Gabriel, flaws and hauntings and all. But only if he loved her back.

"Angelique? Baby? Am I wrong? We don't have to do this." Gabriel's concern and Emmanuel's discomfort finally registered.

She shook her head, smiling. "I'm fine." She looked up at Emmanuel. "Really. I'm fine."

Gabriel winked at her, relief making him seem almost lighthearted. "That you are. Isn't she, Manny? It should be a sin to cover up a body this delicious."

Angelique laughed, shaking her head at his teasing, and caught Emmanuel staring at her breasts with a hungry expression.

Gabriel rubbed her thigh in approval and she cupped each heavy globe in her hand, lifting them as if for inspection. "Is this what you're looking at? Would you like to touch them?"

She wasn't sure how she'd gone so quickly from submissive to brazen, but Gabriel didn't seem to mind.

Emmanuel looked to him for permission, and whatever he'd seen must have let him know it was okay to move closer. He sat down beside her on the bed and she touched his sleeve. "Why don't you take off your jacket? I'll feel weird being the only one . . . naked."

As soon as she'd said it his long jacket and whatever shirt he'd been wearing beneath it disappeared like magic, leaving him in only jeans, boots, and the most unique assortment of tattoos she'd ever seen.

He was unreal. BD-beautiful, but more vulnerable. His tousled hair cried out to be stroked. His blue eyes made her want to cry. His body made her want to cry for another reason. There was nothing vulnerable about him there. He seemed to be molded from muscle, his back and arms slightly larger than Gabriel's.

The tattoos were unusual. Like black scars with stitching holding him together at his shoulders, his chest, along his spine.

It made him appear even more unearthly. The markings were strangely heartbreaking. She wanted to ask him about them but she didn't want to spoil the moment.

"Thank you, Emmanuel."

He smiled, almost bashful, though he still had a hard time keeping his eyes away from her cleavage. "You can call me Manny."

Gabriel snorted and stood up, stepping back, but Emmanuel didn't look up at his reaction. His hand lifted, then hesitated, above her breast.

Why did he seem so uncertain? Surely he couldn't be . . . She looked up at Gabriel, silently asking the question. He nodded.

Unbelievable. And, with the way Emmanuel was looking at her, incredibly flattering. She would be his first. His first *every-thing*. The idea sent a stream of heat through her veins, melting her nervousness away.

She took his hand and placed it on her breast, carefully watching his reaction.

A flush darkened his cheeks. The deep, impossible blue of his eyes glittered with surprised desire. His fingers tensed, his palm scraping across her nipple, and she arched slightly in reaction.

He noticed. He did it again, massaging her flesh, learning her, focusing only on her. She turned her body more fully toward his, licking her lips in anticipation.

"Can I kiss them?" Emmanuel's question was to Gabriel, she knew, as much as it was to her.

Please say yes, she thought in his direction, surprised she was finding this innocent exploration of her body so sensual.

It hit her that he had been alive in a time where she would be considered a harlot. A wanton. That somehow made this all the more thrilling.

Gabriel didn't let her down. "I think she'd be insulted if you didn't. Be gentle with your teeth, at first, until you discover how much pressure it takes to make her wet."

The hand on her breast froze and Emmanuel looked at her. She nodded. "Please."

He bent his head to her free breast and kissed the top curve with his soft, gentle mouth. He trailed a blazing path of achingly light kisses along the side, just beneath her nipple, and the freckle that marked the start of her cleavage. *Homage*. That was the only word for so thorough an exploration of a single breast.

It was setting her on fire. It was a sweetly painful kind of torture she wasn't sure she could survive. Angelique lifted her hands to his head, impatient.

"He's a natural, isn't he, baby? He's not even trying and you're already there. Willing. Aching."

Emmanuel lifted his head at Gabriel's words, his blue eyes nearly black now as he studied her face.

"Yes," she told them both. Wanting Emmanuel to know how he was making her feel. Wanting to tell him she needed more. "God, yes."

Gabriel came to stand beside her, his hips at her eye level, his erection pushing against the fabric of his pants. "He needs you to show him, Angelique. Show him what you want."

He slipped his hand inside his unbuttoned pants and pulled out his thick cock, pressing the slick head to her lips. "Show him."

Angelique kissed the tip of his erection chastely, knowing Emmanuel was watching her every move, his hand still massaging her breast.

She opened her lips and took Gabriel into her mouth, her tongue slipping out to swirl along his shaft, making him groan.

"That's what she wants. She wants you to taste her. Wants you so hungry for her flavor that you take too much."

She moaned in agreement and sucked him deeper, lowering her head until she'd taken as much as she could.

Gabriel's voice was gravelly as he continued. "Wants you to suck her nipples against the roof of your mouth. To pinch them between your fingers a little too hard. Oh, fuck, Angelique. Like *that*."

She cried out against Gabriel's flesh when she felt Emmanuel's mouth open over her nipple. He *was* a natural. His teeth gently bit down; then she felt the scrape of his tongue as the fingers of his other hand twisted her nipple with just the right amount of pressure.

Angelique squeezed her thighs together, trying to ease the ache by rocking her hips back and forth. Emmanuel's mouth left her nipple and she almost shouted in dismay until she felt it on her hip. On her stomach. The tops of her thighs. Oh God.

She got up on her knees on the bed, her legs spread wide as she continued to lift and lower her mouth on Gabriel's erection.

"Not asking my permission anymore?" Gabriel sounded more aroused than upset. "Lie down on the bed with your head between her legs."

She sensed movement and then he was there, his hair silky against her thighs. She lowered her hips until she felt the first brush of his lips against her sex.

There was no more room for shyness, no more words of instruction. He didn't need it. After the first swipe of his tongue, he moaned low in his throat, his fingers tightening around her thighs. And then he was feasting. Sucking the lips of her sex, licking her, filling her with his tongue.

A memory of the other night in the kitchen doorway popped into her mind. Emmanuel watched Gabriel do this to her. He'd seen it. Had he fantasized about it? Touched himself? She thought he could taste her fresh arousal when he pulled her closer as though greedy for more.

She lifted her mouth off of Gabriel's cock and shouted as she came. He held her steady as she pumped her hips helplessly against Emmanuel's mouth, unable to control her body.

When she was done quivering, Gabriel lifted her off Emmanuel and into his arms, growling when the younger man tried to reach for her again. "Back off. She's addictive, I know. But back off."

Emmanuel stilled, watching him carefully. They were both like wary animals. And she was the bone.

Angelique caressed Gabriel's shoulder, and he started to relax. She kissed his neck. The line of his jaw. Loving him without words.

"You liked what he did for you?"

She nodded against Gabriel's temple, kissing him there as well.

"Do you think he deserves a bit of reciprocation?" Gabriel leaned away from her mouth to snare her gaze. "And I'll be inside you to make sure he doesn't distract you too much."

She nodded again, unable to stop her smile.

Gabriel grumbled at her. "Those dimples would let you get away with murder."

Emmanuel had gotten off the bed, still hesitant to move closer, but clearly tautly strung. Gabriel positioned her so she was kneeling on the bed again, this time with him behind her.

She reached out for the waistband of Emmanuel's jeans and tugged. When he was close enough, she looked up at him with a warm, impish grin and looked at the denim. "Bet you could make those disappear, too."

Before she could blink, he'd complied. "Oh, my." He was breathtaking.

She glanced over her shoulder at Gabriel, who was sliding on his condom impatiently, and laughed.

He spanked one ass cheek without cracking a smile, but his green gaze sparkled with humor and . . . affection? Love? He took her hips in his hands and fit the head of his cock inside her, his size making her breath come out in a pleasure-filled rush with the first shallow thrust.

She turned back to Emmanuel, taking him into her hand with a gentle grip. His thick lashes flickered, but he didn't look away. And neither did she.

Angelique kissed him gently, tenderly. Light strokes of her tongue took in his taste. His scent was clean and bright. Like green grass and sunlight. Like Emmanuel.

Time seemed to disappear. All she knew was desire. The delight of watching him experience this first, intimate kiss. The pleasure and ecstasy she felt as Gabriel took her to the place only he could. Passion.

Emmanuel never reached for her, his fists digging into his thighs as she brought him to the edge. He went over with a soft cry that was nearly drowned out by her moans and Gabriel's raw shout of completion.

Gabriel pressed his forehead to her shoulder, her name a shaky murmur on his lips. But her eyes were still on Emmanuel.

She wondered how someone could look so satisfied, yet so lonely at the same time. She wished she could soothe him.

He bent down beside her and kissed her. Humbly. Gently. Then pulled back and smiled. "Thank you, Venus."

And then he was gone. Again.

Gabriel didn't say a word; he just tumbled her backward, pulling the covers over them and cuddling her close.

She closed her eyes, suddenly exhausted. As she drifted into sleep, she could have sworn she heard someone calling her name.

Angelique.

* * *

SHE WOKE UP A FEW HOURS LATER, LISTENING TO GABRIEL'S slow, steady breathing, trying to calm her own.

She couldn't; something was wrong. She couldn't shake the feeling that something was off. It was so strong she had to extricate herself from her lover's grip and get out of bed.

Angelique. Come.

Walking over to her clothes piled in a small heap in the corner, she saw it. The locket, glinting with unnatural light.

She put it on without thinking, feeling its warmth against her skin.

Your mother would be ashamed. She needs you and you aren't there.

Her mother needed her? Was that the foreboding that had woken her out of a sound sleep? She didn't question it. She threw her clothes on and walked out of the room, knowing there was no time to wake Gabriel. No time to tell him what was wrong. She had to go now.

Stepping outside just as dawn was breaking, Angelique started to walk. She was heedless of the sounds and movements of the waking city. Of the men sleeping in alleyways along her route.

She had to get home.

Sin. You spent a night of sin while your mother was in need. Just like your father. Weak like your father. Can't resist the darkness. Your brother, your mother, they know. Know how like him you are.

How could they not know? It was so obvious to her now. It was why they'd always watched her so closely, always worried. They knew what was inside her. That she was just like him.

She stopped in the street. Shaking her head as if to clear it. She was nothing like her father. Her family knew that. She knew that. Why was she thinking this way? Maybe Emmanuel was nearby. Could he find out if her mother was safe? "Manny?"

How can you still resist me? Resist the truth? How is it even possible? You are full of doubt. You proved how weak you were last night. Ran back to spread your legs for the same man who'd used you and lashed out at you. You would keep him bound to you if you could. You would sell your soul just like your father did, hurt your friends. Hurt your mother. All for a man who doesn't even love you.

He hadn't said that he loved her. Not once. She'd seen something in his expression; she knew she had. It felt like love, at least the beginnings . . . but he had never said it out loud.

And then he shared you with someone else. Don't you know, little girl? You're just his whore. A whore for a man who embraces dark magic, consorts with voodoo spirits, and steals your will. It is the same magic that your brother had to suffer through. Your family had to pay for. You are your father's daughter. You are cursed.

She *was* cursed. Or her family was. Why had she thought she'd gotten off scot-free? Her father's crimes had been too ugly. He'd gone too far. Her brother had spent years suffering for it. Her mother had spent most of her life alone, with no love for herself. Angelique was no different. She was worse, because she hadn't understood. Hadn't helped to ease their pain.

She crossed the street and saw the same man from the bar last night. The one she had seen before. Bloodshot eyes stared unblinking. He made no move to follow her, just watched her as she walked swiftly away from him. Why was he watching her?

He warned you, didn't he? But you won't admit that he was right and you were wrong. Always wrong. Go home now. Your mother is looking for you.

She made it to her apartment, though she wasn't sure how. As she walked up the steps, she felt different. As though she wasn't in charge of her movements. They felt jerky. Alien. Like a dream.

The door was unlocked. When she opened it she could see her mother sitting on the couch, a cup of coffee in her hand.

Theresa Rousseau stood up as soon as she came in, looking relieved. "I was wondering where you were, Angelique. I know I shouldn't have used the old key; you deserve your privacy. But I haven't seen you much these last few weeks and I thought I'd surprise you with breakfast."

She narrowed her eyes as she studied her daughter's wrinkled dress and wild curls. "Are you all right? What happened?"

Angelique wanted to reassure her mother, but the words wouldn't come out. Instead she walked over to her and hugged her. Too tightly. Why was she holding her so tightly? She focused on relaxing her arms.

"Baby, what is it? What's happened to you? Did someone hurt you?"

Angelique's mouth opened and words she hadn't planned to

say came out. "They tried, but I'm protected; you know that. Remember when I was little, when I was scared you told me you'd made sure nothing could hurt me? Why am I protected, Mommy? Why can't Daddy's darkness touch me?"

Theresa looked at her oddly, but she patted her arms and nodded. "I can't believe you remember that."

"Why am I protected?"

"Your cross. The priests at the Catholic church blessed it."

"Not just the priests."

Theresa was trying to move from her arms now, obviously unsettled. "How did you know that? I never told you your aunt Cecilia blessed it as well. She insisted . . . just to be safe."

Angelique stepped back swiftly. "Aunt Cecilia. The Santeria priestess? She's nowhere near powerful enough."

"What?"

"I don't think it's working. I'm scared. We need to go see the Mambo. I'm worried something dark is after me."

"Angelique, my dear, please. What is it? What is after you? Why do you sound so strange?"

She turned around and felt a vague sense of horror when she caught her expression in the mirror. Her expression, but not *her*. As if someone else was watching through her eyes. Something else.

Her arms reached up behind her neck and she unclasped the cross she'd never taken off before. "Call them all, Mama. Michelle and Allegra and Mrs. Adair. Tell them we'll meet them at the Mambo's house. It's an emergency. Trust me. I think my life is in danger."

She wasn't sure how her mother responded. The last thing she remembered was looking at the cross in her hand, watching her fingers uncurl, and feeling the chain slide across her skin until it slipped, tumbling to the ground.

After that she started to scream until everything went dark.

CHAPTER 14

GABRIEL SLEEPILY SLID HIS HAND ACROSS THE SHEET, searching for Angelique's soft form. He'd had another nightmare. The darkness that had been chasing him was after her as well. He needed to feel her press against him, hear her heartbeat. He needed her.

His body stirred as the scenes of the evening replayed in his head. She'd been incredible. He may have been fulfilling her fantasies, but she'd surpassed his. And she'd done something more. She'd gotten past his defenses. The young, sassy Angelique had gotten to his heart.

"Morning, Sugarpants. Did you sleep well?"

BD's syrupy drawl was the only warning he got before he

was dragged out of the bed and slammed against the wall so hard the wind was knocked from his lungs.

"What the—"

"Rousseau, you agreed to restrain yourself."

Gabriel kicked Celestin's kneecap, then pushed him away when his grip loosened in surprise.

Gabriel put his hands on his thighs, bending over to catch his breath. This was *not* how he wanted to start his morning. "Damn it! BD? Rousseau? What the hell are you two doing here?"

And where was Angelique?

He looked up. Celestin Rousseau was a big man. The tattooed and dreadlocked older brother of the woman he'd spent all night defiling. With her permission, of course.

But obviously not Celestin's.

"Not happy to see me, you bastard?" Celestin snarled, taking a menacing step in his direction.

BD stepped in front of him, keeping a firm hand on his shoulder. "Rousseau, calm down."

"Fuck you, BD. I trusted you to have my back, my family's back, but you just couldn't resist bringing my baby sister down to your level. And *Bethany*. I can't believe she knew and didn't—"

"*Enough.*" BD's expression changed dramatically. So dramatically Celestin took a step back. "No one, not even you, my friend, speaks disrespectfully about my wife."

He turned a gaze like amber fire on Gabriel. "You should probably put your pants on before the interrogation. Angelique's friends are in the other room, but I don't think they'll be kept at bay for long."

He reached for the khaki pants at the foot of the bed, grumbling. Her friends, Ive and Kelly. Where had they stayed last night? And how had they gotten in? "What did she do, send out morning-after invitations?"

Celestin growled at his muttered words, but he kept his distance.

BD sighed, still watching Celestin through his lashes. "They spent the night with Bethany and me, and now they refuse to go home until they find out what you did to Angelique. They also, it seems, called her brother. Who called Benjamin. He should be here any minute. There is something going on Gabriel. More than you are aware of."

Gabriel felt his face heat. Jesus, he had to get out of here. And what did BD mean, what he'd done to Angelique? Did they want a blow-by-blow? "Why don't they ask her? Isn't she out there? What the hell *is* going on?"

"Would we be here if she was out there?" Celestin's expression was grim. "You shouldn't have been here with her in the first place. Ben told me you were reckless, not stupid."

BD rolled his eyes. "Of course, Benjamin is the perfect role model for sanity in matters of the heart. And you've *never* behaved like an ass for love. Bah. I can name five instances now off the top of my head."

"Love?" Celestin gritted through his teeth, glaring at BD. "She's just a baby. An innocent. None of this ever had to touch her. All this time he's been making everyone miserable, making us feel *sorry* for him and causing his mother pain. But he's been too busy fucking around with my little sister to worry about that."

Gabriel stood and zipped up his pants. Celestin was right. He'd been a grade-A asshole to his family. An asshole to repay the kindness Rousseau and the others had offered by sneaking around behind their backs. They deserved better; that wasn't news.

He'd take any lumps they gave him; he deserved it. But he wasn't going to apologize for Angelique. Not when he knew that, given the chance, he'd do it again.

Celestin wasn't done listing his sins. "Last night he dragged her out of the club like a Neanderthal, away from you and her friends without a word. Now while he's sleeping peacefully, she won't answer her phone and no one has seen her."

"Wait. What?" Gabriel was awake now. He pushed past the two men and stalked into the front room of the suite, searching for some sign that she was here.

Ive and Kelly were standing by the window. They both jumped when he appeared.

"Where is she?" Gabriel knew he sounded gruff, knew he looked angry, but he couldn't help it.

Before they could answer the hotel door opened and Gabriel whirled around, heart in his throat. It was Ben Adair and Bethany. They both looked worried. Shit.

"She's not at her apartment. All I found was a cup of cold

coffee and this on the floor." Bethany held up the small cross that Gabriel had never seen Angelique without.

BD swore and reached for the necklace. "Blue Eyes, this is not good."

"None of this is." Bethany noted Gabriel's half-naked body and sleep-tousled hair and sighed heavily. "I don't mean to join the mad mob here, but I have to ask. Angelique is too important. Did you black out again?"

He felt the others staring in judgment. Angelique's friends no doubt thought he was a drunk, or a lunatic. But he just avoided them and shook his head, his expression earnest. "No. I had total control of it this time. I swear to Christ, Bethany. I fell asleep with her in my arms. That's the last thing I remember."

The doubt coming at him from all sides was taking an almost physical form. More shadows. It ate at him, made him doubt himself. What if he had hurt her? How could he have taken that kind of chance, being with her after having taken in even the smallest amount of darkness?

Maybe he'd been too rough and she hadn't said anything, leaving after he'd fallen asleep. Or maybe she hadn't liked what he'd let Emmanuel do to her.

Or had his nightmare come true?

"Emmanuel. He was here for some of last night. He could tell you." Gabriel looked around, expecting to see the guardian who'd shared in Angelique's pleasure appear in the already crowded room.

Celestin sneered. "Blackouts? Has he been drinking again

along with everything else, BD? And why the hell is he calling for Emmanuel? What—does he think he can see ghosts now?"

Gabriel refused to acknowledge Angelique's brother. "Manny, you get your ass in this room right now." His voice was hoarse with worry. "Don't fuck around. This isn't about you; it's about her. *Where is Angelique?*"

He felt crazy. He was crazy. He'd pushed her away again and again. Wanting to save her from what he'd become, wanting to save himself from having to watch her crush turn to disgust when she saw him for what he really was.

Now all he wanted was her. He loved her. And she was the only damn person in Louisiana not in this hotel room. The only person who might believe him if he said those words. Who might say them back.

Bethany touched his arm lightly. "Emmanuel had me look into something he said she had. Something she shouldn't have. That might explain this; I don't know. I do know with all of us looking, we'll find her." Her blue eyes, so like her brother's, shone with compassion. "I believe you, Gabriel."

"Well, I don't." Celestin came after him again but Ben intercepted him, swearing as his cell phone started to ring in his pocket. Everyone froze.

He reached for it and swiftly put it to his ear. "Any news? Thank God." He paused, his expression going from relief to concern as he studied the other people in the room. "I understand. I love you, too. Hang in there, Mimi."

Everyone started talking at once, but Ben ignored them and

pulled his fist back, sending a short but power-packed punch into Gabriel's jaw.

"Fuck." Was *everyone* going to punch him?

He landed hard on the floor, cupping his jaw, while Ben stood over him and Celestin just looked stunned. It hurt, but the pain was nothing compared to the fear that wound around his heart.

"Angelique is at Mambo Toussaint's," Ben announced in a clipped voice.

Bethany knelt down to help Gabriel up. "They found her? Then why did you hit him?"

Ben crossed his arms, his expression unapologetic. "It's a family thing. Someone was going to do it. Better me than Rousseau." He smirked. "He hits harder."

"No rules saying I won't still have my turn." Celestin's tone had lost some of its anger and his eyes reflected the same relief Gabriel felt.

In fact, Gabriel's own knees were weak with the feeling. "Then she's okay?"

"In a minute." Ben turned to the two women who were clinging to each other, watching the exchange in silent fascination. He placed one hand on each of their shoulders. "Ive? Kelly? Angelique is fine. She will be fine. The best thing you can do for her right now is to go home. We have a family situation, but once that's resolved, I'll make sure she calls you. Understand?"

Ive looked into Ben's eyes for a long moment, then nodded. "Come on, Kelly, get your things."

Kelly resisted. "I don't have the best feeling about this. Shouldn't we—"

"No."

"But can't we just—"

Ive grabbed her friend's hand. "*No*. She's not dead, she's not missing, and she's with family. A magical, *secretive* family who doesn't think we could help our best friend out of whatever it is that she's involved in." She looked at Kelly meaningfully. "The voodoo police have arrived."

Kelly glared at Ben. "Well, I don't like it."

Ive gathered their scattered clothes and makeup bags from the bathroom. "I don't, either, but now is not the time."

Celestin smiled when the two women walked up to hug him each in turn. "Angelique is lucky to have friends like you."

The echoed "We know" had Gabriel looking on in bemusement.

Ive hustled Kelly toward the door, looking over her shoulder at Gabriel. "Take care of our girl. And if you ever make her cry again, you and the most interesting parts of your anatomy will have to answer to me."

The other men cringed beside him, but Gabriel nodded. "I won't. I promise." It was one he intended to keep. Or die trying.

When they left, everyone turned to Ben.

"What's wrong?"

"Angelique is at Mambo Toussaint's . . . and so are the others."

BD tilted his head, on high alert. "Which others?"

"The Mambo, Allegra . . . *my mother and my wife*. And the

222

way she told us to come over, BD. I don't know. Something is very wrong."

BD gripped the cross tighter in his hand. "Something is very wrong, Benjamin. Too many coincidences. All of them centered around Gabriel and Angelique."

The tone of BD's voice set Gabriel in motion. "You don't believe in coincidence. And neither do I anymore. Let me grab my shirt and we'll get—" He bent down to pick it up off the floor and stilled. "Out of here."

The carpet beneath his bare feet had turned to cobblestone. The sound of a brass band nearby came to him on a sweet breeze, along with an aroma so mouthwatering that Gabriel's stomach rumbled.

He looked up. Blinked. Looked again. He was alone on a side street in the French Quarter. No friends in sight. No hotel room.

He slipped his shirt on, not bothering with the buttons as he studied the buildings around him, trying to understand what he was seeing.

This was no blackout.

It was New Orleans. Only it wasn't. The streets were too clean, the paint too fresh, the sky too blue. Hell, even the scavenging pigeons seemed to glow with a pure, unreal kind of light. This was a romanticized version of the Crescent City.

A dream?

"Emmanuel?" Gabriel turned slowly, looking for someone, anyone, who could explain this to him.

"Manny, if you're messing with me—"

A little African American boy dressed in a short-panted suit that looked like something out of the nineteenth century was standing at the edge of the street. He was looking directly at Gabriel.

The noise of the trombones and trumpets grew as the band he'd been hearing began to march and dance in unison past the child. The whole scene was disturbingly surreal.

"Hello? Can you see me, kid? Do you know where I am? Do you know Emmanuel?"

The boy's dark, soulful eyes continued staring. He didn't move, didn't react. Gabriel's eyebrows lowered. Had he not heard him?

When the last of the small parade of players passed, the child smiled, pointing down the street in the direction they'd gone. And then he ran after them.

"Really?" He looked up and raised his voice. "Follow the band? That's the only clue I get?"

His angry stride ate up the ground beneath him, heedless of the stones digging into his heels. "Son of a bitch. I don't have time for this. Not that I know what *this* is." He shouted at the backs of the jazz band preceding him. "Do I need to sing it? Angelique may need me. I. Don't. Have. Time for this."

No one was listening. He kept walking, feeling like he was heading to his own funeral. Maybe he was dead. If so, they were marching him in the wrong direction. Uptown.

He thought about the last few weeks. How much had changed since he'd come home. Other than everybody and their older brothers punching him, it hadn't been bad. Hell, it had been fucking fantastic. At least, whenever Angelique was around.

He could see a future now. Maybe he even wanted it. One where he had people in his life he could count on. Where he was somebody someone else could count on.

Angelique.

She was the piece holding all of that together. Without her, he knew, it wouldn't work. God knew why she wanted him. What she'd seen when she looked at him that he couldn't. He didn't deserve her, but he was just bastard enough not to care.

He stopped walking and stood in the middle of the emptying street. "I'm not playing this game. I need to get out of here, now."

He grabbed a handful of rocks from the ground and turned to face the perfect, empty candy shop. Complete with large glass window. "Let me the fuck out or I will start messing up your pretty little world!"

An ethereal female voice stayed his hand. "No need, Gabriel. We have always liked your energy and enthusiasm, misguided though it may be, but we'd rather not have to clean up any more messes today."

Gabriel turned, closing his fingers over the stones instead of dropping them. "Am I dead?"

It was a question he was suddenly taking more seriously. How else could he explain the threesome that had appeared before him?

Two women, both long-haired beauties with perfect bow mouths and skin that practically glowed in the sunlight. Identical in every way but the differing colors of their antebellum gowns and parasols. They stood on either side of an old black man with a white beard, a straw hat, and a walking stick. And they were all smiling at him.

Dead or dreaming. He wasn't sure which.

The old man chuckled. "You're not dead *or* dreaming, son. You're a Toussaint."

Gabriel was thoroughly confused. "Well, I'm kind of new at being one, though I'll admit you do look familiar. Can you give me a break and let me in on the joke?"

"Of course I look familiar." He tipped his hat jauntily on the side of his head. "You've seen me before . . . and you will again. More important, you've seen these lovely ladies. Unforgettable in every way."

He stepped back and bowed as if to present the women at his side. They giggled.

"Flatterer." The one in blue blushed.

"Rogue." The one in green batted her thick eyelashes at the older man.

Gabriel's mouth formed the words before he'd realized he was saying them. "The Marassa Twins?" That would make the old man . . . No. No, it couldn't be. The keeper of the crossroads? The being who had helped Ben find his sister in time to save her when the *djab* had possessed him?

"Got it in one." Papa Legba smiled. "They told me you were clever. You just got yourself lost on the road, is all. To be fair, some of the losing wasn't your fault. Luckily you've had some help to get you right again."

Emmanuel? "You sent him to me."

"Not me. I am not authorized to make those kinds of ar-
rangements." His expression was enigmatic. "Emmanuel and I
are working toward the same end, though I didn't send him. We
both wanted you to find your way home for our own reasons."
He looked up as if talking to the sky. "Only Bondye, the good
god, knows the reason why we couldn't work together."

Papa Legba huffed. "He's a good boy, that Manuel, and I
feel for him. I surely do . . . but he's got a bit more time to find
his way. And he has been helping—he's helping now. But it's *you*
we're here to talk about."

The Loa. He was talking to the keeper of the crossroads and
the Loa twins who'd had made his sister *bon ange*. "Why? I
mean, why now?"

After all this time. After all he'd been through. Italy. Father
Leon. The *djab*. Why were they talking to him now?

The old man's smile carried a tinge of sadness. "Would you
have listened, child? Would you have even heard us?" He shook
his head as though he already knew the answer. "The bad is
always easier to believe than the good. Because of that, it took
something as dark as that *djab*, took what almost happened that
day, to get past all the walls you built up around yourself.
Around your gift."

What was he saying? That he'd had it all along? Bullshit.

The woman in blue slid back her parasol and looked into his
eyes. "A male Toussaint, rare indeed. A twin to a *bon ange* as
well. He would need a powerful gift to protect the sister who
sees, to protect the people he loves. A child wouldn't be able to

handle that kind of power. It would only come to him as he grew, strong and secure in the knowledge that there is light as well as dark. Love as well as hate. And how to use them both in balance."

Her twin in green began to speak as soon as she was done. "That kind of power would have to be balanced carefully; its foundation is in love so it couldn't be used to destroy and snuff out the light in the world. Used for war or vengeance. Or used against the user himself."

Gabriel backed away, shaking his head. "It never came to me. I didn't grow up knowing *light* and *love*. I grew up believing you were all just demonic illusions. That my sister was evil. I didn't protect her; I almost—"

"We know, child. We know. But now so do you." Papa Legba patted the women's hands comfortingly and stepped away from them. He moved closer to Gabriel and lowered his voice. "Isn't that what you were just thinking? That maybe you could get past your past? What is true for you is true for everyone walking your world; if you close yourself off to love out of fear or hurt or pride, you block everything that comes with it. The blessings of your family, your gifts, your strengths. The light."

The old man looked down at his open palm and made a fist. "Everyone around you has been telling you the same thing. Bitterness doesn't make you strong. It shuts itself up tight in the dark, keeping you from seeing what you could be. What you should be." He opened his fingers. "Love is your key. Love makes the light break through the darkness. She is your light, destined for you as surely as the sun is destined to rise."

The kindness and understanding in the Loa's bright eyes tightened Gabriel's throat with emotion. Love was his key. He'd known it. Loving Angelique set him free.

"Angelique." He gripped the old man's shoulders and looked at the women behind him. "I need to get back. Do you know what's happening? Where she is?"

The three laughed politely and Gabriel's expression turned rueful. "Stupid question. I sincerely apologize. Can you tell me? Is Angelique in trouble?"

"Bethany knows." The woman in green smiled. "Ask her about the locket." Her expression sobered. "And yes. Your Angelique is in trouble. More than she should have been. The others have gotten desperate. No innocent was allowed to be brought in. We suspect foul play."

"Foul play? The others?"

Gabriel watched Papa Legba catch her eye meaningfully and she sighed. "We did not offer this power lightly. Toussaints have always been loyal and powerful believers, worthy of our gifts. Your family is a force of healing and good in the world. You can be, too. But not all the Mysteries believed a mortal could handle such power. Deserved the power. Still others desired it to be used for a darker end, which is not what *we* intended at all." She took a breath, obviously distraught at the idea. "Those others believe if Angelique's influence is removed, you would never be able to control your gift. Never find balance. And they could use you for their own purposes. Or watch you destroy yourself."

Papa Legba patted his shoulder consolingly. "They don't know how strong Toussaints are."

Gabriel stepped back abruptly. "No disrespect intended, but why do I suddenly feel like a piece on a fucking chessboard? Isn't this my life? Don't I get a say? And what does Angelique's influence have to do with any of it?"

Papa Legba soothed the woman beside him, shaking his head at Gabriel. "Careful, boy. There are things in this world you don't understand, nations and families of Loa who rarely see eye to eye, but you have one thing right. It *is* your choice. You've always had it. The Marassa offer you a gift, but whether you use it for good or evil is up to you. There will be choices down the road, important choices and powerful consequences. Consequences that affect everyone. Even here. But today's, I think, is the most important choice for you. You love her."

It wasn't a question. "Yes, I do."

The old man nodded. "If she were lost and made to suffer, you would seek revenge?"

"Yes."

He sighed sadly. "Then they would win. They have been there all your life, boy. Poking holes in your heart and shaking your faith. The last thing they wanted was for you to come home, to find her. Find love. Those meddlers always lusted for battle and destruction, and that has its time and place, but they are wrong about you. You are no Dark Messenger. Not

Gabriel Toussaint. I have faith in you. And I know you can save her."

Save her from what? The locket? Angry Loa? He felt like falling to his knees in pain, ready to beg them. "Please, you have to send me back. I have to help her."

Papa Legba backed away from him slowly. "Yes, you do. In fact, I'm afraid you're the only one who can. They made sure of it. They don't think you're strong enough yet, and that is their mistake. They think they'll win. It's also why we made sure you came here first."

What? If he had to sacrifice himself, he would. "Anything. Tell me what to do."

The two women shared a look and then began to walk toward him simultaneously. He couldn't move. His feet felt as though they were glued to the street. What were they doing to him?

He heard Papa Legba's voice over the rushing sound in his ears. "They give you again what was yours from birth, Gabriel. Light and dark. Love and hate. You can see it all now. See it . . . and use it if there is a need. Use it to protect your family. For Angelique."

The Marassa Twins reached him, both standing on tiptoe to press two perfect bow mouths to either cheek. Their whispers echoed in his ears. "Our gift to you, brother of *bon ange*."

The sky that was too blue and the grass that was too green started to swirl together like a ruined watercolor. And still, Gabriel could not move.

"Hurry to her now, Toussaint." Papa Legba's voice seemed to come from far away. "And welcome home."

"HE'S OPENING HIS EYES. GABE? GABRIEL, WAKE UP." BETHany sounded anxious.

Gabriel opened his eyes and looked around. He was lying on the floor by the window. The hotel room. He was back. His shirt still clutched in his hand. "How long was I out?"

BD, leaning against the window ledge, looked over at the clock. "A few minutes only. Did you hit your head?"

"No, he didn't."

Gabriel looked down at Ben's hand on his arm and sighed. "Never could keep anything from you. Not even when we were kids."

Ben dragged him up to a sitting position. "I saw it. Holy shit, Gabe, I saw it. And heard. I had no idea—" He shook his head roughly, obviously trying to clear it. "We can talk about that later. If they were right, which is a given, we need to leave now and get Bethany to tell us what she knows. Can you stand?"

"Yeah. I'm fine. We need to go."

His head was spinning. And—he rubbed his eyes—everyone looked . . . off. Like he'd stared directly into the sun before he'd looked at them. He would think he was still in Loa land if his jaw wasn't hurting again.

Bethany looked up at the men around her, a frustrated sound emerging from her throat. "Who? What? When? What did you see, Ben? What just happened? Did someone mention me?"

BD smiled down at his wife. "I'm betting they saw Papa Legba, Blue Eyes. The one who used to lecture *me* all the time on interfering." He sighed, shaking his head. "I must have been a good influence."

Gabriel nodded, slipping on his shirt for the second time. "And the Marassa Twins. They said . . . a lot of things. Most important, that Angelique was in danger, and if the other women are with her . . ."

A sound of gut-wrenching pain emerged from Celestin's throat. "Allegra and the baby."

Gabriel strode ahead of them out the door. "We need to get to my mother's as soon as possible, and, Bethany? On the way, you need to tell us about that damned locket."

CHAPTER 15

WHERE WAS SHE? WHY COULDN'T ANYONE HEAR HER?

Angelique had woken from her darkness into a new kind of hell. She couldn't move her arms or legs. Couldn't feel them. Couldn't feel anything.

She heard muffled sounds behind her. Wailing sounds that terrified her, made it hard for her to hear what was going on in the world outside of herself. The world she saw through what she could only describe as a wavering window smeared with streaks of mud.

Oh God, what was happening to her?

Through the window she saw herself taking her pale, trembling mother by the arm and walking all the way to Mambo Toussaint's, ignoring her mother's stumbling as she attempted to keep up.

"Mama, I'm so sorry."

The Mambo greeted them warmly at first. Until she saw Theresa's face. Then Angelique noticed concern change her expression.

"Mambo! Help me!"

So far, only a few people had come in answer to Theresa's call. Elise, Michelle, and Allegra were sitting in the living room.

She hoped they stayed away.

Looking relieved to see her, Michelle got up off the couch and swept her into a hug, but Angelique couldn't feel it. Why didn't she see?

"It isn't me."

Before Elise Adair could touch her she backed away, making the older woman frown and ask what was wrong. But by that time it was too late.

She moved to stand behind the armchair where the very pregnant Allegra was sitting, stopping her sister-in-law from turning to look at her with a clawed hand in her hair.

That was when she saw the knife. The carving knife from her kitchen.

"No! It isn't me. Don't hurt Allegra!"

"They can't hear you."

She knew that voice. "Emmanuel? What's happening? Where are you?"

He sounded worried. "I'm as near to you as I can be."

Angelique tried to think past her panic. "You need to go. Need to help Allegra. Tell them it isn't me. Oh, please, Emmanuel. Help them."

His voice took a soothing tone. "Help is on the way, Angelique. Gabriel is on his way. It won't make its move until it has what it wants. Otherwise, it would have already killed your mother."

"Oh God!" Killed her mother? And Gabriel was coming?

This was Hell. Being forced to watch everyone you love look at you with horror. Watching as you hurt the people you care most about in the world.

"Shhh. I'm more worried about you. You have to fight this." *Emmanuel's voice turned hard.* "Trust me, I know this place. You can get back some control if you focus. I'm going to show you how."

She was crying but she couldn't feel the tears on her cheeks. "I can't. I can't move. I'm trapped."

"You can. You're a bright soul, Angelique. A strong and beautiful soul. That's why it had to work so hard to overcome you. I'm sorry I didn't see it before. Didn't protect you."

It. Something. Something had overcome her. Taken her over. Like Gabriel?

"Is it a djab?"

Emmanuel hesitated. She wished she could see his face. "I'm not sure, Angelique. I only know it's old; it has some awareness. And it's very angry. I shouldn't have left you alone last night. I should have known, or taken it from you before you ended up here. If I'd been doing my job . . . I should have taken it."

Taken what? "Where is here?"

"That paper-thin barrier between life and death. Before you reach the crossroads. Before you can move on. It is the space of a heartbeat for some, eternity for others." *He paused for a moment, as if weighing what to tell her.* "The screaming you hear? Those are the trapped and lost. They aren't souls. They are torn pieces. Fragments. Not whole like you. They exist here in rage and in agony. They reach for the souls that cross over, desperate to touch life. To remember life. It is not a place anyone conscious would want to be."

He sounded painfully familiar with this location. Had he been trapped here? Was this where he was after he left Bethany last year?

"How did I get here? What happened?"

"I think it was trapped in this place. And that the locket kept it from escaping somehow. Whatever happened, whatever it is, it's trying to rip your soul apart, but we can't let it succeed. Without a soul, you can't live or die or be reborn. You cease to exist forever. And I won't let that happen. Not to you."

Cease to exist? "Why?"

"It can't completely take over until you are gone. Either it doesn't know how or it's weakened from its imprisonment, but the longer it stays, the stronger it will grow."

"Why didn't it just take me and hide? Why is it trying to hurt my family?" She was having a hard time taking this in. How the necklace, something that seemed so innocent, could have done so much damage.

"Fear makes you weaker. Maybe it thinks if you are afraid of what it will do, you won't struggle. It doesn't want you to fight back. It wants to live. To feel. It will do anything, including threatening the people you love, claiming abilities it doesn't have . . . Anything. We can use that desire in our favor, its lust, but I need you to trust me."

She did trust him. And she wasn't willing to give up. It had succeeded in scaring her; she wouldn't lie. Even now she was having a hard time not joining the screaming voices in the distance.

But it had underestimated her and made a mistake if it thought she would fight harder for herself than she would for her family.

"What do I have to do?"

* * *

"Why can't Michelle send it away?"

"Because it isn't a soul. Not really."

Gabriel listened intently. What Bethany had told them was already terrifying.

According to her, after Emmanuel had talked with her about what he'd seen at Angelique's, she'd gone back to the journals. One of them had a picture inside. An aged, sepia-toned picture of a woman wearing the locket.

She'd read every entry last night, her horror growing with each turned page. It told the story of a New Orleans family of hougans and mambos. A lineage of powerful priests and priestesses going back to Haiti, as long as anyone could remember.

The author of the journal had inherited the home, as well as the knowledge that her ancestors had strayed far from the path.

Bokors, dark priests, had dwelt in the house. Bones were found in the basement, as well as other macabre signs of sacrifice. Bloodstains were hidden behind painted walls. And something unnatural roamed the house at night, getting into the new owner's head. Into her heart. Scaring her and her young husband so much, they nearly lost hope and each other.

When all of the artifacts had been destroyed, and no smoke or sage ritual could seem to cleanse the house of the evil, they called in help.

A hougan and a mambo agreed to work together on her problem. She gave them one of her great-grandmother's lockets to use as a lightning rod, something the energy would recognize.

They told her that all the evil done in the house had left a mark. A stain of greed and malice, jealousy and wicked intent. It grew so strong that it became aware of its own existence. It was alive, but all it knew, all it wanted, was to create more of what it was. More fear. More pain.

Bethany spoke softly. "She said they performed a three-day ritual, sending everyone away from the house. When she returned, the mambo appeared ill and weak, and the hougan handed her the locket, wrapped in a scarf. He said they weren't strong enough to disperse it, that they'd had no other choice. They trapped it."

Ben was rubbing his temples as they turned on the final street to Gabriel's mother's house. "She never destroyed it? Sold it?"

"She was terrified," Bethany reasoned. "It must have been like owning Pandora's box. I suppose one of her children must have inherited her things, then died, leaving no one behind. That's how it came to be at your mother's shop."

Gabriel wanted to hunt down whoever had sent this to his mother. Wanted to scream at the arrogant beings who had his Angelique open the box it came in. Made her take it home.

His Angelique. His fault. They'd done it to hurt him through her. By taking her away.

"We're here." BD pulled into the narrow parking spot and turned off the car. "I should have known something was up when I saw that man being ridden last night. Damn, this makes me wish I could borrow back my Loa powers for an hour or two."

Ridden? "Possessed? Do you think it was watching us? Angelique?" Was it one of the Loa who wanted to hurt her?

Rousseau growled. "Of course he does. He doesn't believe in coincidence."

"Amen," Gabe murmured. They all sat in silence for a moment, and then he rubbed his face roughly with his hands. "They said I was the only one who could do this, so I should go in alone. There's already too many people in there."

"Fuck you, Gabe." Ben reached for the handle of the car door. "My wife is in there. Our families."

"I second that. Fuck you, Gabe." Celestin, who'd been crowded into the backseat with Bethany and Gabriel, already had one leg on the curb.

BD put a hand on Ben's shoulder. "We will all go. All but Bethany."

"Excuse me?"

Gabriel watched as BD turned toward the backseat, a look of determination crossing the handsome man's features. "I love you, Blue Eyes. I'm not ordering you; I am *begging* you. For the sake of my child inside you, stay in the car."

His child?

Celestin looked up at BD, understanding and apology in his eyes. "I agree."

Bethany's stubborn expression had melted with her husband's words, and her hands unconsciously cradled her still-flat stomach. "Okay."

Gabriel opened his door as the other men got out, but turned when Bethany whispered, "BD is only human. Don't let him forget that."

"I won't."

He frowned as he walked toward his mother's familiar door. He wasn't sure what he was supposed to do, or how he was supposed to do it. If people trained to handle this sort of thing had failed to disperse it, what chance did he have? Hell, he knew more about exorcisms than he did about voodoo.

He had to trust in what he'd seen, what Papa Legba had said.

"Manny," he muttered. "If you're listening, I could really use your help right about now."

The door was open. Gabriel went in first, the unnatural quiet sending a jolt of fear down his spine. The four men walked in silence to the living room. Where he'd had that first, awkward reunion with his family. Right before the *djab* had taken him.

It was also where he'd first seen Angelique.

Now he turned from the hallway to the living area, seeing her again. Silently holding a knife to Allegra's throat.

He saw Ben and BD immediately reach out to hold Rousseau back. Good. He didn't think startling Angelique would be the smartest move right now.

Angelique. Not Angelique. Still wearing her dress from the night before. And the locket around her neck . . . was open.

It smiled through her when it saw him. Had it been waiting for him? He saw the others from the corner of his eye. All of them watching, unblinking. Confusion and fear and anger coming off them in varying shades of shadow that he could see. Could use.

"You shouldn't have come," Michelle spoke in a tight whisper. "I thought you'd understand."

Ben's chuckle held no humor. "As if I wouldn't, Mimi. You know better."

Angelique's voice sounded high. Strange. "I will trade her for him."

Gabriel focused on it. It made a motion with Angelique's hand and he understood. "Me for Allegra? Deal."

Angelique's expression became suspicious at the easy victory. "Why?"

Of course it would be confused. It didn't know positive emotions. All it knew was fear and betrayal.

A familiar voice whispered in Gabriel's ear. "Don't speak; just listen. Angelique is still alive, but we have to hurry. We need to distract it with feeling. Lust. It used her lust for you, and her doubts to free itself. But you can trick it. Seduce it. Angelique wants you, so it will, too."

Emmanuel? Thank God. Seduce it? The thing that was consuming her? He hoped like hell Manny knew what he was talking about.

"Why?" It was turning shrill. Bringing the knife closer to Allegra's neck.

Gabriel shrugged. "Does it matter?" He took a step closer, his hands out, smiling. "Don't you want to have me at your mercy?"

It hesitated, its glassy stare sliding up and down his body

before nodding sharply, allowing him to move closer. He closed off his feelings for the other people in the room. He had to focus.

He studied the energy around it. Light and darkness. Love and hate. He could see both. That meant Angelique was still there. But he wasn't sure for how long.

He maintained his smile, though a part of him wanted to cry out that she had to suffer this at all. Suffer like he had. No control. No power. "Take the knife away from that woman. She means nothing. None of them do. Only you and I. Let me help you. Take me."

The thing in Angelique looked confused. "I have her memories. She fears for them."

"Ah, but what she feels for me is more interesting than fear, isn't it? Look at those memories. What I've done to her. Aren't you curious? Don't you wonder what it would be like to experience that with me?"

All his attention was trained on Angelique's energy. He was looking for an opening. Looking for a sign.

"I know you want her," he crooned seductively. "I want her, too. We could share her body. Together."

Angelique's face flushed. It recognized the lust Angelique's body had known. Was responding to it. The hand holding the knife lowered, allowing Gabriel to lift Allegra from her perch and place her behind him.

"Gabriel." BD's words held a warning . . . and concern.

He couldn't think about them right now. He stood in front of Angelique, one hand behind him, signaling the others not to rush her. That wouldn't save her. "Everyone should leave now. I want to be alone with her."

He heard movement, the sounds of people rushing out of the room, and hoped his mother and sister had been among them. "See? I can protect you. And I can make you feel things you can't even begin to imagine."

She held the knife against his chest, pushing just enough to prick him with the sharp tip. He looked down and saw a small circle of blood form on his shirt, and smiled.

It's Angelique. Her body. Think of Angelique.

Gabriel rocked his hips forward, pressing his stirring erection against her body. "I could play hostage if you'd like. You can force me to pleasure you at knifepoint. Or I could just turn the tables on you now and get it over with."

Gabriel's hands whipped up to grip her wrists, twisting them behind her back and tightening until the knife fell harmlessly to the floor.

It smiled and the darker energy grew. He recognized it. Felt it move in his direction. Everything he'd been running from. The twisted lust. The violent darkness. He'd have to embrace it all now if he wanted to win.

"You like that? I knew you would. Would you like me to tell you what else I know?"

He leaned closer, ignoring her snapping teeth and whispering in her ear. "I know this body loves to be spanked. Loves to be made to submit."

A desperate sound of excitement emerged from Angelique's throat.

Gabriel held both her wrists in one hand, tighter than he would have under normal circumstances, and pulled up the back of her dress. "I know I can make it just painful enough to feed your hunger."

He rubbed his palm threateningly across the cheeks of Angelique's ass, taunting the creature with something it wanted just out of reach.

It jerked against him in frustration, trying to get away. He laughed. "Oh, did you want to be the one doling out the pain? Knowing how it feels to watch them kneel at your feet, begging you for it?"

Its eyes lit up. "Yes."

"Well, baby, you picked the wrong body. You want that power? Want to cause that kind of lust, that kind of pain? Then you need someone stronger."

"She's strong. I could cause you pain."

He tightened his grip on her, bending her backward until she cried out. He whispered against her temple. "I'm stronger. If you really wanted to, you could have me. I won't fight you. I want you to." He pulled back just enough for it to see his eyes. "Or are you too afraid?"

He let himself go for a moment. Let the ugly, bitter memories, the hate and rage that had been a part of him for years, swell inside him.

Like to like, as BD had said.

It recognized itself in him. And the impatience, the desire, inside it flowed toward him like a black molten river. The intensity of the shadows that swirled around him, inside him, were difficult to resist. Heady. Powerful.

There was no going back now. He let it in.

He could see nothing but darkness. It gorged itself on what was inside him. His punishments. His sins. The Dark Messenger with all the power of a demonic god. But he wanted more. He wanted all of it.

Gabriel sensed the moment of triumph as it left Angelique slumping in his arms, the moment it began to push him out of his body. For a heartbeat he was afraid it would succeed.

Love is your key, Gabriel. Love makes the light shine through the darkness.

He heard Papa Legba's voice as if the old man were right beside him, and suddenly he knew exactly what to do.

Angelique? I love you.

He opened up his heart where he kept his memories. His mother, rocking him back to sleep after he'd had a bad dream. Playing with the sister, who was his best friend, his heart. All the love he'd kept locked away, hidden from the world, he showered on the darkness.

The energy balked, its movements confused. It was afraid.

Gabriel turned his thoughts to Angelique. She was his beacon. She was why it wouldn't win. Why they, whoever the hell they were, wouldn't win. He loved her. He chose her. He may doubt himself, his worth, but he didn't doubt the strength of his feelings for her.

Every secret longing in his soul, every ounce of love he had to give, he gave to her freely, allowing himself to feel that for the first time. He belonged to her. He would love her until he died.

When he saw that light glowing inside of him he realized something. He hadn't been stealing energy from her. Emmanuel had been wrong, but Bethany knew. It was her. Angelique. She'd been giving it to him all along. Asking for nothing in return. She'd loved him.

Like to like.

He watched as the light permeated the shadow, bursting through like sunlight after a storm. The darkness had nowhere to go. No understanding of it. No sanctuary from it. In him it had made its last stand. And lost. Love swept through him, washing away every foul emotion, every bitter regret. Until nothing of the darkness remained.

He dropped to his knees with Angelique still in his arms, his shaking arms laying her down on the floor beside him. Her lashes flickered weakly.

"Angelique? Can you hear me, baby?"

He felt a hand on his shoulder. "She'll be fine now," Emmanuel said. "And so will you. You did it. You figured it out and saved her."

Gabriel shook his head. He knew he hadn't done it alone. Despite what the Loa had said. "We did it."

He leaned down and kissed her forehead, talking softly in case she could hear him. "You did it, angel. Loving you saved us both."

* * *

"I WISH YOU'D TOLD US."

Gabriel smiled and reached for his sister's hand across the kitchen table. She was grumbling, but he could hear the underlying concern, the love, now. With Angelique resting safely surrounded by her family in the other room, he finally let himself relax. "I'm sorry, Mimi. For everything."

He watched Ben place a comforting hand on her shoulder and squeeze. "Not to ruin the moment, but I'm still wondering what Papa Legba meant about what was coming down the road. And why your gift makes everyone on the other side so jittery."

Annemarie Toussaint set a towering plate of johnnycakes onto the table. "We heard the story, but we'll deal with it later. Stop talking now. My son needs to eat. Saving us all from a horrible death must work up an appetite."

Gabriel stood and took his mother in his arms, ignoring her exclamation of surprise. "And I'm sorry I brought this into your house, Mama. The last thing I ever wanted to do was hurt you. I love you."

She looked up at him and her beautiful eyes filled with tears. He had been such a fool not to tell her that sooner. "I always have, even when I thought you'd sent me away."

"Oh, my baby boy, you're back, aren't you? You're really home." She hugged him so tightly he wondered if his ribs might break.

"She thought you might blame her for letting Angelique sneak out with that locket in the first place."

The Mambo lifted her head to glare at Elise Adair, but the older woman just shrugged. "What? You did."

BD finished chewing the corn bread and shook his head. "Everyone knows it wasn't her fault. Mambo Toussaint is powerful, but these Loa were trying to stay beneath the radar. Still, I don't think they'll be back anytime soon. Not after the show Gabe put on today."

Gabriel watched the stubborn expression on her mother's face find its mirror in Michelle's. "We'll make sure they don't."

He smiled. "My family. I am a lucky man."

"Don't get too nice too quickly, boy. You might strain something." BD came to stand beside him and held out his hand. Angelique's cross was dangling from his fingers. "And never let her take this off again. Theresa belongs with the Mamas more than she knows. This is as powerful a gris-gris as any I've seen."

So was love. Gabriel grinned. Damn, he was being poetic again. And he didn't care. He was still sure he was right.

He looked over at his sister and his smile widened. "Someone else hug me before I turn into the grumpy twin again. You know it's just a matter of time."

CHAPTER 16

ANGELIQUE STEPPED OUT OF THE SHOWER AND REACHED for a towel, humming her favorite Bessie Smith song, "Do Your Duty."

Gabriel had certainly done *his* last night. She giggled at her reflection in the mirror. Not that he was ever unwilling. Or uncooperative. Or unhappy.

In fact, she could hardly think of a time in the last few weeks when he hadn't been there to see to her every whim and desire before she even knew she had it. And he did it with a smile.

It was freaking her out.

She stuck out her tongue at her mirror image. She was just being difficult. She'd wanted him to love her. And she was gloriously happy.

He'd just been so . . . *gentle* with her. And she knew why.

She'd be lying if she said she'd escaped what happened unscathed. If Mambo Toussaint hadn't made that batch of sleep-good tea, she wouldn't have closed her eyes at all those first few days.

At first, Celestin had taken her to her mother's house, putting her in the room she'd decorated just for her. Bethany and Allegra had come to visit, as well as Ive and Kelly, but she couldn't talk to them. Couldn't explain where she'd been or what it had felt like to be trapped there—looking out.

She'd needed Gabriel.

After three days she'd called BD and told him to send Gabriel, repacked her small bag of things, and waited. Her brother had come over, trying to convince her that she needed to stay with family. That Gabriel couldn't take care of her.

But when he'd driven up to her mother's house and come to the door, Celestin hadn't stopped her from going with him.

He'd purchased a house only a few blocks away from Bethany and BD's. The only furniture consisted of three boxes he'd had shipped from Italy and a bed.

Gabriel had carried her up to his bedroom and held her in his arms, rubbing her back until she'd fallen asleep. It was the first peaceful moment she'd had since that thing had taken her over.

She'd been here ever since.

Angelique had told him everything. Everything she'd felt and seen, her horror when she realized that the body that was supposed to be hers was threatening the lives of the people she loved.

She knew he was the only one who would truly understand.

Her brother had been the host of a mischievous, sexual spirit. She knew he'd suffered. Knew it didn't matter what you were taken over by, just that you were. Now more than ever she felt for what he'd been through. But only Gabriel understood what evil felt like. And only through his eyes did she see that she had no reason to be ashamed. That it wasn't her fault. He showed her the light.

Now she would have to remind him that there were a few things about the darker side that weren't all that bad. Especially the way they did it.

The sounds of male voices raised in argument made her frown. She reached for her short, terry-cloth robe and slipped it on, trying to tie the belt with one hand while she opened the bathroom door with the other.

"It's been weeks. There is no reason why she should still be here."

Her brother. Of course.

Gabriel's voice was steady. "I think she can be wherever she wants for as long as she wants. It's up to her."

Angelique could practically hear her brother tearing out his hair. "Don't tell me about my sister. I don't care what you can do or see. I've known her all her life. I know she can. I'm saying you can't just . . . well, just *live* together like this indefinitely. She's special, too. She had plans. She has a future."

Top of my class, she quipped to herself. She should announce her presence, but she didn't yet. Old habits died hard. She really felt for Celestin. He always tried to do the right thing. Mama was probably driving him crazy with the "living in sin" speech.

Gabriel's words made her hold her breath. "I agree."

"You agree. With what?" Celestin asked suspiciously.

"All of it." Gabriel sighed, the first sign of his own frustration. "I won't stand in the way of her future. I know she told you about the engineering job she got with the city. The one she took to stay in town. And I know what you're getting at, Rousseau, but I'm not the person to talk to. I know how special she is. I love her. She's it for me. And I've asked her every day for the last two weeks, but—"

Angelique continued walking down the hallway, unable to contain her smile. He loved her. "But I've said no." She caught Gabriel's green gaze and winked. "For the moment."

Celestin looked down at her and shook his head, his shoulders slumping. "I have a hard time believing we were raised by the same mother. Theresa Rousseau? Remember her? Remember the 'Why buy the cow when you can get the milk for free' speech? Any of that ringing a bell?"

Angelique laughed and threw her arms around her brother. "I love you for defending my honor. I really do. But you have a baby coming, literally any minute now, and I think you have more important things to focus on than my marital status."

Celestin squeezed her back, kissing the top of her head the way he always did. "Nothing is more important than you're happiness, little one."

She leaned back and let him see her face. "I am happy."

He looked at her, then toward Gabriel. "I can see that."

"Good." She grinned. "Now go home. Give Allegra's belly a kiss for me."

Celestin nodded, his goofy smile at the mention of his wife's rounded stomach making her snicker teasingly.

When the door closed behind him, she turned to face Gabriel, arms crossed.

Gabriel held up his hands, looking innocent. "What? You heard me. I was nice to him."

"Yes, you were nice."

"Why are you looking at me like that?"

She let him see the need in her eyes, felt it heat her limbs as she leaned against the door. "You need to stop it. Now."

"Stop what?"

"Stop being so damned nice."

She watched Gabriel's beautiful face flush. His strong jaw tightened; his mossy green eyes dilated. Beneath the T-shirt she'd bought him because he owned only stuffy button-downs, his muscles rippled visibly, reacting to her words.

He knew what she meant. He'd made love to her with all the fire and passion any woman could desire. But he'd held himself back, not wanting to go too far. Not after what they'd both had to go through. Not now that he was so aware of the light around her, and still not entirely used to dealing with it.

But she loved him. Everything he was. The power and the vulnerability. The good and the bad. And she wanted exactly that. Everything. Gabriel when he was nice . . . Gabriel when he was naughty. If she had to entice him, to tempt him, into getting both, then she would.

She touched the belt around her waist, moving to open it.

"No." His voice rasped.

Damn, he had a sexy voice. "No?"

His smile was wicked. "I'm glad you picked out such a sturdy table."

Oh yes. "In the dining room?"

"Yes. I want you to go over there, take off your robe, but lay the belt on the table. Then I want you to bend over it and wait for me."

The belt? What was he going to do with the—

"Baby, did you hear me?" Gabriel's voice was gentle, but deliciously commanding.

"Yes."

She walked a bit unsteadily toward the dining room. Her heart was beating so fast she felt light-headed. The fluttering in her stomach increased when she saw the thick plank table he'd asked her to pick out for him. Other than the bed and some books and paintings, there wasn't a thing in this house he hadn't wanted her input on.

She slipped off her robe, her hands shaking as she unlooped the soft fabric and laid it on the table. When she felt the smooth, cool wood against her breasts, she breathed out a laugh. She hadn't imagined this when she'd picked it out.

Liar.

"Are you laughing, baby?" Gabriel came up behind her, his shirt off, that familiar sparkle in his eyes. Thank God.

"Only if it means you'll spank me."

*   *   *

Emmanuel watched them from their open window. They were lying on the couch, lost in each other. He knew the conversation they were having was an intimate one. Knew he should announce himself or leave them alone . . . but he couldn't tear himself away.

They'd been like this since they'd gotten back from Ben and Michelle's house, witnessing the birth of a new Rousseau. A little girl Celestin and Allegra had named Ariel.

Another angel.

Gabriel was apparently taking the opportunity to press his case for marriage.

"What if I promised to spank you every day?" Gabriel asked.

"Tempting, but no." Angelique choked out a laugh when he tickled her in punishment.

"Sing you boy-band songs?"

"Nope."

"Give your favorite werewolf-loving professor a grant?"

She smacked his arm playfully. "Hey, no mocking. You and I both know anything is possible now. You told me Emmanuel said—"

Emmanuel watched Gabriel place his fingers over her lips to silence her. His charge slipped off the couch onto his knees, looking up into Angelique's eyes.

He had to strain to hear what Gabriel was saying. "What if I told you that I love you? I want to grow old with you, have babies that our mothers can spoil rotten with you? That before you I was lost in the darkness, until . . ." Gabriel looked around her and Emmanuel knew they saw the same thing. Angelique's bright spirit. "Until you found me, drove me crazy, and made me happy for the first time in my life. Then would you marry me?"

Angelique was crying. She lifted her hands to Gabriel's face and gifted him with a smile so radiant Emmanuel almost felt the need to look away.

She shook her head.

Emmanuel's jaw dropped as Gabriel pulled away from her to stand. "Damn it, Angelique."

She got to her feet as well, reaching out for his hands. "What if *I* told *you* that I love you? That I want to grow old with you and, if it's in the cards, have babies like Ariel that our mothers can spoil? What if I told you that you are the greatest adventure I've ever had, one I want to be on until I die . . . and hopefully after." She laid her hand on his heart. "A piece of paper and a white dress doesn't guarantee anything—you know that as well as I do. Both of our fathers proved that."

He frowned at her, but Emmanuel could tell he was listening. "Nothing is guaranteed, Angelique. But I can wait for you to think about it. I think."

He leaned down to kiss her, his smile disarming. "Though I reserve the right to tempt you into changing your mind, if only to honor your mother by—"

Angelique gasped with laughter. "If you say by buying the cow, you are so going to pay for it."

Gabriel picked her up and headed toward the bedroom. "BD is right. It's worth it. You're worth it. Whatever it takes. Some-

ABOUT THE AUTHOR

R. G. Alexander has lived all over the country and has studied archaeology and mythology, has been a nurse and a vocalist, and is now a writer. She is married to a talented chef who is her best friend, her research assistant, and the love of her life. Visit her website at www.rgalexander.com.